Born in Italy of Hungarian parents, Inez Baranay migrated to the western suburbs of Sydney, where she was educated, then moved to the inner city. She has been a schoolteacher, traveller, compulsive shopper, television researcher, scriptwriter, editor and journalist. Her short stories have been published in many modern anthologies. *Between Careers* is her first novel.

IMPRINT

BETWEEN CAREERS

INEZ BARANAY

Collins
Publishers
Australia

To Milena

IMPRINT

COLLINS PUBLISHERS AUSTRALIA

First published in 1989 by William Collins Pty Ltd
55 Clarence Street, Sydney NSW 2000

Copyright © Inez Baranay 1989

National Library of Australia
Cataloguing-in-Publication data:

Baranay, Inez.
Between careers.
ISBN 0 7322 2522 1.
I. Title
A823′.3

Typeset in Times Roman by G.T. Setters Pty Limited, Kenthurst, NSW
Printed by Globe Press, Victoria

Cover illustration:
Philosophies of the Boudoir: Dangerous Relationships by Julie Brown-Rrap

Creative writing program assisted by the Australia Council, the Australian
government's arts advisory and support organisation.

'. . . let us ponder all the ruses that were employed for centuries to make us love sex, to make the knowledge of it desirable and everything said about it precious.'

Michel Foucault

Acknowledgements

Thanks to Sasha Soldatow for a thorough and generous editing job on an earlier version of *Between Careers*. Thanks also to Dianne Harris and Lucia Bibolini, who gave me a home in Rome in 1979, where I was able to write full time.

The *Coda* was written with the assistance of a half-year New Writer's Fellowship from the Literary Arts Board of the Australia Council, the federal government's arts funding and advisory body.

The two quotations from Michel Foucault's *The History of Sexuality* (Volume One) were translated by Robert Hurley and originally published by Allen Lane.

Contents

PART ONE

1

The Truth about Violet

It is strange to think that Violet might have played a part in anyone else's life, just as if she were real. Violet was only an invention but she had her own existence. Vita should know where she came from and what happened to her, but Violet did not have a neat beginning or a neat end.

It's hard to remember her clearly. Her kind come and go. Vita looks into a mirror for clues, she tries to make the expressions Violet would have used; all she sees is a silly grimace then an impatient, disbelieving scowl. Violet would not have scowled much. Cheerful, willing smiles would have been more her line.

Recalling Violet, you would see her in the dark back seat of a taxi, being driven through an over-lit night to her next appointment. She dabs more powder onto her face, recollects her part, ready to win the next round, ready to play as if each time were new—the given sequence: the telephone, the taxi, some unknown man waiting, the money, the make-believe sex, leaving him behind.

Violet was considered interesting because of her profession. Why was it said to be the oldest, as if money were invented primarily to purchase the imitations of men's secret dreams?

If anyone knew her, it would have been Vita, although she may not have fully understood Violet's motives. Maybe it was simple: Violet wanted to be rich and bad.

Violet disappeared when Vita could no longer keep her out of her own life. She had to be a separate person.

2

Breathtaking Views

She could never remember all of them, but there were some who made an assault on her memory. There was Libra. He had a special arrangement with Pamela. He did not like to discuss money with her girls, and the business side of their relationship was never to be mentioned. He would come to Pamela's office and pay her the cost of two or three bookings including 'extras', so he had credit. Then he would ring up when he wanted someone. And it was always this late, Pamela said, instructing Violet on her first date with Libra. It was 2 a.m. But it was all paid for.

'Just don't mention anything about money,' Pamela said. 'And don't wear your black dress. He likes girls feminine; once he sent a girl in a black dress home for looking like a vamp. Wear your light blue.'

He was a drunk who lived in a large, brand-new apartment with breathtaking views of the ocean. He led her to the balcony where she exclaimed extravagantly at the sea, the stars, the moonlight on the dark waves, the pleasure of hearing that rich ocean sound.

'I don't suppose you appreciate this,' he said, as if she had said nothing. 'Most people wouldn't appreciate this.' He slurred his words and left out syllables, in the manner of a stage drunk.

'I appreciate it like mad,' said Violet.

The inside of the apartment was breathtaking too. It was the most perfectly hideous contrivance of expensive bad taste she had ever seen. And that, as they say, is really saying something.

He was drinking port and went to pour some for her. Their first date was one of the most trying few hours she had ever endured: that said the same something.

'Could I have a whisky, please?' That's the way you always put it the first time.

4

'We're drinking port.'

She took the glass, sipped, then left it. She could be stubborn too. And she decided to stay sober.

He was thirty-two but looked older, a short, fat man with a bloated face and thin, ginger hair. Then he told her the saga of his marriage break-up: the wife who had divorced him, the children he was not allowed to see. It had been a long time ago—they had married straight out of high school. He went back sometimes for a day's business to the town where the school and the marriage had been, and he would look at all the kids coming out of school, he told her, his voice thick, and wonder which of the boys were his. That was the only story he ever disclosed about himself. She never figured out if it was meant to account for his evident determination to drink himself to death. The story took a long time as he kept repeating parts:

'You probably don't want to hear this.'

'Of course I do.'

'You probably don't believe this.'

'Of course I do.' Why not?

'You're a very nice woman,' he slurred. 'I need a woman to understand me. I'm a Libra,' he announced, 'and a Libra needs a woman who can understand him and not call him something because he wants to have a drink.'

'I'm a Libra too,' Violet offered, brightly, casually. It wasn't taken casually. It was the first thing she said that he took notice of.

'You're a Libra. A Libra woman. I've been looking and looking for a Libra woman. Only a Libra woman can understand a Libra man. Libras are the most beautiful people in the world.' The same words lurching at her over and over.

'Yes, they are,' she obliged. She wouldn't have known. 'Tell me more about Libras.' Something new for Violet to use.

'Libra people are the most beautiful...aren't they? A Libra would never hurt anyone...would they?' And so it went. Soon Violet would learn that the less a client could do for her—or she for him—the more grateful he would be. As he insisted on her responses she began to get a clue how to deal with

5

him. And time was getting on. She asked for the bathroom (chrome and glass: more taste) and then to see his bedroom. There it was, his bed—Italian velvet bedspread, satin sheets, fancy blankets. Unmade.

Violet submitted to him and his clumsy fumbling and groping. It would be fruitless, but she had to wait for this, his withdrawal from the battlefield. Unarmed as he was, it was necessary to establish faith.

With a kind of fierce, even hostile, triumph, he produced a vibrator. An electric one, with cords, plugs, different speeds... Was this to nullify his impotence; to make reparation with an orgasm machine that would bestow its credit on him? No man about town need rely on flesh and blood alone.

This was no time to reflect or theorise. She played indifferently with the vibrator for a while to assure him she was not left high and dry. She wasn't there to amuse herself. But he needed to be soothed, not aroused, so she distracted him.

She murmured into his ear. She told him he was safe. All was well. She murmured hypnotically of his sweetness and of peace all around. Men were often lulled to sleep by assurances that at other times they would call lies. And that's all he really wanted, this coarse, rich drunkard: a good night's sleep. It's all a lot of people want. Empires of religion, therapy and pharmaceuticals are built on the promise of that one true lullaby.

He dozed off quickly. In the bathroom, Violet took one of Pamela's cards from her bag. She reapplied her lipstick and pressed an imprint of her lips on the card which she then left propped against his shaving cream. She dressed, tiptoed around and telephoned for a taxi, while he slept.

A week later, very late at night, Pamela was on the phone. 'A request for you,' she said. Violet didn't recognise the name at first.

'He seems to think he's found someone very special; he earbashed me when he came to pay. I had to get rid of him, he would have stayed for ages.'

'He's no fun either.'

6

'Go and see him. Oh yes, he was grooving on about some card you left—what was that?'

She told Pamela about the lipstick signature.

'Cute, eh?'

'He liked it,' Pamela said, 'but not enough to pay any extra. Half an hour?'

3

Men Like That

Violet had just come from a double booking with another of
Pamela's girls. The two men had a regular Friday evening together.
They always had a few drinks after work. Then they would check
in to two rooms at a good hotel and telephone for a couple of
girls. They liked to meet different girls each time—inevitably they
'couldn't afford to get involved'. That's why they ordered girls
instead of meeting them at parties.

Every Friday evening was the same: the four of them would
have dinner in the larger room, their 'suite'. (Room service, because
they 'couldn't afford to be seen' either. And it was more informal,
they would say, taking off their ties.)

'Make yourselves comfortable, girls.'

The girls would kick off their shoes and cross their legs. The
business was left to one of the team. He would pass an envelope
to one girl. The girls would politely have a drink before going to
the bathroom together where they would count out the money and
divide it, and maybe whisper, 'Which one are you having?' while
the men outside whispered the same. The money was enough if
dinner didn't take ages, and it wouldn't. Another inevitability was
the men's order of Great Western champagne to drink before and
during the meal. There was no after—once the food and drinks
were away they were forgotten.

The girls would obligingly twitter and giggle. Waiting for room
service, they would compare nail polish and ask the men what kind
of business they were in. The men would be hearty and jolly. It
passed for a good time. Then everyone would mess up the stuff
on the metal trays as quickly as possible and the girls would pour
Great Western into the ice-bucket and the oyster plates when the
men weren't looking. Then the girls would get as sexy as anything.
By now it was clear who was assigned to whom. If natural

attraction failed there was a subtle pecking order which gave the dominant man and the dominant woman first choice of each other. The token dinner out of the way, one couple would head for the other room.

'See you in a while then, mate,' the men would call archly.

The two left in the suite would abandon the mess and move to the adjoining bedroom. Violet would take her time, undressing showily—something had to take time. She would join him in bed. Minutes later she would be back in the bathroom. Only magazines and textbooks talk of afterplay. His orgasm was his proof that he'd got what he'd paid for. 'Not yet,' he would beg and she would lie outwardly still, as if in an attempt at prolongation, but her well-exercised skill would soon have him groaning in mixed pleasure and regret. Or whatever it was.

When she came out of the bathroom, he would be putting on his socks, ready to go home to his wife. He would hand Violet a tip—that would be to show that his expense had been a bliss in proof. Then he would go to meet his mate again, perhaps, and they would have a last drink before heading home, each of them making sure the other knew he had really gotten his rocks off and given that chick the time of her life. 'I'm buggered now, mate,' they would say suggestively, as an excuse to leave each other. Neither would admit they had been mad in pursuit of a swallowed bait.

Maybe that's how it went. How would she know? Violet had left behind another hotel room, another faceless, nameless number, and all considerations of his inner mind's workings.

Waiting in the corridor for the hotel elevator she was joined by Simone, the girl who had shared the dinner. So, she had taken the same time—maybe there was an established standard duration. They flashed mild but genuine pleasure at the sight of each other. No post-coital *tristesse* for ladies of the night. So much richer, and about to be home nice and early for once.

'What a living,' Simone remarked with voluptuous satisfaction. 'Isn't this the easiest money you ever made?' It certainly seemed that way at times. They were alone in the elevator which kept on stopping though no-one got in.

'What amazes me,' said Violet, curious for a second opinion, 'is that they are satisfied with that. They do that every week. Do they think that's all sex can be?'

'Men like that have no idea,' Simone said, beyond contempt or caring.

'Buying sex could never be as good as making love with someone you like,' Violet probed, 'so why do they act like it is?'

'I suppose you'd have to see their wives...'

The wives, whoever they were, had no existence for Violet. She failed to imagine them. Who made the beds they lay in?

4

Obscure Desire

The question was whether to go out again or not. Libra's request. Well, a job's a job. But Libra? And there'd be no tips or gifts— business was not to be mentioned. Strange how Violet felt less reluctant setting out for a blind date than when she was going to meet someone she knew. Still, there was no good reason to refuse. Not feeling like it is never the point.

'I know he's a hassle,' Pamela said encouragingly. 'He rang for you the other night but he didn't have any credit left. He was wild, got all insulted because I wouldn't let him pay afterwards.'

Great.

Seeing Libra proved a lesser ordeal each time. There was no need for the bitter, garbled narrative of his failed marriage or the sour allusions to the league of destructive women who had shredded his self-esteem.

There was a new litany:

'You really wanted to see me too, Libra woman.'

'Yes, yes.'

'Libras are the most beautiful...'

'Yes, they are...'

'A Libra woman would never say you can't get it up...'

'No, she wouldn't...'

'Libras understand each other...'

Patience! Whoever introduced him to these scant astrological notions had a lot to answer for.

He was always drunk and somehow more easily tranquillised by her every appearance. She would lead him to the bed and stroke him and croon the narcotic lullabies of assurance. She didn't understand Libras at all but she faintly understood what *he* needed.

She would listen to his noisy breathing, poised still, the sweet thief, ready for flight. She always imagined that he might wake

11

five minutes after she'd gone and become furious at her defection. After all, she'd never made him do what it was assumed she was there for.

But how could he say that all he wanted was a pair of tits to lay his head on and a female hand to stroke him and a soft voice to ease him to sleep? There's no name for all that. Buying a fuck must have seemed the only way to recapture a feeling of the cosy, accepting warmth that, whether or not it had ever existed, he sought to regain. And so, wondered Violet, stumbling into her taxi, sex is not always passion, it is so many different things.

These are modern times and sex is easy to ask for. It's a lot harder to recognise that you might really crave affection adventure comfort attention rebellion approval punishment—whatever; an unexpressed longing which is supposed to be achieved in sex.

The taxi turned a corner. So there is a kind of reverse sublimation around these days, she thought, watching the sleeping houses through the smeared windows of the cab. Once, all the things people wanted were supposed to demonstrate sexual sublimation, but now that sexual explicitness is commonplace and fucking *de rigueur*, sex is required to transform and eliminate more elusive longings; to silence hints of obscure desire; to stop a despairing infantile screaming that not even the bottle could silence; not even the rhythmic, magical ocean sighing and shushing below.

You're allowed to think these things at three o'clock in the morning.

5

Taste and Distaste

Violet's new world was filled with businessmen. They provided most of Pamela's clientele. Unlike some of Pamela's girls, a few of whom had formerly been secretaries to such men, Violet had not known or thought much about that kind of man before. One of these former secretaries had turned up at a hotel room with a recently-adopted new name and found herself awaited by, yes, of course, her former boss. The rest of the story went like this: they got over the shock, hit it off and had a good time together. He promised not to tell any of the others back at the office.

That happy ending is incidental; in such a situation you would normally be justified in sinking through the floor, or fleeing before he has a chance to look hard enough to make sure it really is you.

Vita used to think men in business were the types who read *Playboy*, voted Liberal, had a wardrobe of expensive suits and ties and moved in a man's world of power, ulcers and golf clubs. She believed they lacked taste. Worse; they lacked distaste. But soon she had to relinquish her right to very much distaste, too. Those unconsidered assumptions might have been narrow and unimaginative, but the picture did not change much. There were exceptions. Exceptions mean nothing.

Most of the men came from out of town—another state, or overseas. When there were conferences Violet would meet pediatricians one week, international Rotarians or something another week. She never knew what this thing called business was, what rites took place in the masculine realms of conferences meetings inspections profit-transactions negotiations. After a day of *business* the visiting merchants traders capitalists investors and travelling salesmen wanted to take a girl out to dinner and then to bed. Or they wanted to have a girl in their bed late at night. They weren't going to miss an opportunity for an illicit screw on a night away from their wives, and call-girls didn't need to be won before or gotten rid of after and the expense account took care of it anyway.

Sometimes business associates would end a day of meetings and deals with a Night Out Together. Pamela would then send a duo, trio or quartet to meet two, three or four men and there would be cocktails first and then dinner at the hotel's restaurant. If somebody insisted on going somewhere else, the girls would declare that the hotel had a perfectly good restaurant; so they would all go there. A falsehood for the sake of convenience. Each girl would then make sure that by the third course her chosen companion had lost interest in the proposed discotheque afterwards and was much more interested in taking her to his room for a quiet drink. It took less time when the room was only an elevator ride away.

During the dinner everyone would talk a lot and laugh immoderately at anything meant to be funny and make sure there was a lot of crude innuendo but no actual crudity. A French girl called Ellie, whose accent sounded stagey but was real, would always order oysters first. Then she'd keep announcing that the oysters were working and everyone would laugh immoderately again. This was the job people called easy money: supplying small talk and immoderate laughter was one of the biggest challenges Violet had met. That, and eating oysters.

If prostitution is collaboration with the enemy, the most reprehensible part of Violet's collaboration was the perpetuation of the lie that there exists a breed of woman whose true vocation is good-time-girl. She never nags; she is never dreary; she never has bad moods; she never demands; she never, seriously, thinks. She finds men fascinating; desires only their approval; glows at their flattery; thrills at their caresses; goes wild for their love-making; never minds their impotence; is grateful for what they give; asks for nothing more and cheerfully leaves when the party is over. And she switches the light off on her way out.

The most amazing thing was that men were not willing to pick up an available girl in a bar, although there were certainly enough of them trying to keep up their minimum weekly orgasm score. The new style get-your-man magazines encouraged women to be taken to bed by anyone vaguely presentable who had bought them dinner. The readers were told, 'You CAN say no', but it was clear that more important were the assurances that you weren't prudish, frigid or unliberated, and you couldn't prove that by saying no. Consequently, there were scores of girls who hung around in bars to make sure they got fucked a lot.

It was bother they didn't want, Violet's clients explained; chatting up some girl and then she might not. And then there was the threat of involvement: if they picked up a girl she'd expect them to call her again, or she'd hang around when they'd finished with her, or she might have problems and become dreary. But if they telephoned Pamela they could meet a girl who knew how to have a good time, who had no hang-ups. And they paid, there were no obligations, they didn't owe anything.

Her clients knew that Violet did not sit in bars waiting to give herself away, that if she wasn't paid first she wouldn't even stay for a drink. They knew she had no choice in who was waiting for her. They had paid so that she would look at them admiringly, laugh at their jokes, listen attentively, and never demur at a movement towards the bed upon which she would groan with gentle pleasure (an imitation of the signs of true ecstasy would probably have scared them witless). And although they paid for her to act out these pretences, they seemed to believe them. People pay for actors to imitate unreal versions of life without wondering what mockery or detachment lies beneath. Violet realised that the acceptance of bad acting on television meant a refinement of her acting ability was usually unnecessary. Whatever most of these men knew of passion could be successfully imitated by the use of lubricant and well-timed panting.

'How do you actually do it?' Vita's friends would ask, the sex part of it, they meant. 'How do you actually fuck someone you might not find attractive?' Well, you just *do* it; you imitate; you pretend. You do exactly what you might with a chosen lover of brief acquaintance, but without the same feeling. The same ritual physical actions are performed. Magazine articles on how to please your husband when you have a headache (and he doesn't) will tell you the same thing.

And, as actors know, imitation is one technique of motivation. If you pretend to cry for long enough and hard enough, making the choking, sobbing sounds of grief, then real tears might come with a strange, real sadness, and it will take some time to recover, to say, 'I was only pretending.' So it is with sex: the imitation of arousal can sometimes create an impetus of its own, enough to make some of Violet's couplings as close as Vita's had been to the Real Thing.

6

The Way it Goes

Vita stays at home, reading, dancing, redecorating, dreaming, dozing or doing nothing. Maybe laying out the Tarot. Maybe looking at travel brochures. She doesn't go out and she doesn't wait, but she has had a bath and done her nails and there's a clean outfit hanging, because she might have to get ready in a hurry. The phone. She has to get ready in a hurry. She takes off everything she's got on. She might have on her silk overalls, or tights and a big paint-splattered shirt, or only a sarong wound around her. First she puts on some fresh, lacy underwear. Stockings if they've been requested, if it's a cool night, if she feels like it. Lots of very good scent. Then one of the useful dresses that once they belong to Violet are worn only by her: the little black, the floaty blue, the elegant cream. Then lots of make-up, more than she'd normally wear. Her hair is fluffed up. And there's a pair of the highest heels she can walk in. Once she steps into them the transformation is complete. The high heels elongate her calves, creating a lovely long curve. They are simply, wickedly beautiful. They symbolise both vulnerability and domination. They make her feel both helpless and powerful. It seems so wrong that they look so lovely and are so crippling, so damaging. Well, enjoy them, my dear, you will never wear them again.

Should it have been the other lipstick, more mascara, less shadow? Don't worry, don't think about it; you'd better go. Violet's bag is ready: all her make-up, credit card forms, lubricant, and a packet of condoms that never gets opened because the odd strange man who wants to use them brings his own. She looks different, she feels different, she *is* different. Don't forget that note by the phone—the name, the hotel, the room number. She sways out the door. She hasn't given a thought to whoever is waiting.

17

She hasn't given a thought to whoever is waiting. She sways through the door. It's held open by a middle-aged American businessman. He is dressed only in a bathrobe.

'Hello, I'm Violet.'

'I know, I was expecting you. Jim Macmurray.'

'I know, I was told. Hi, Jim.'

She swiftly looks about the room to form an impression as she goes towards a chair.

'Excuse my casualness, won't you. I just got out of the shower.'

'That is always appreciated,' she says.

'Can I get you a drink?'

His done-it-all-before attitude makes it easy for her. She acts coyly feminine to make it easy for him.

'Please. Whisky—Scotch I mean—no ice. Where are you from, Jim?'

'Detroit, in Sydney for three days, been here three times before, here on business and I'm in the automobile business.'

Isn't he cute! Isn't he clever! He knew everything she was going to ask him. Now she doesn't know what to ask him.

'Let me ask the questions, then. How old are you? No, musn't ask a lady her age.' He thinks he's funny. 'Have you got a boyfriend?' He hands her the drink.

He hands her the drink.

This one's a bit of a slob, could be a lawyer, that type. He is subtly—probably unconsciously—hostile to her. His hostility is the source of his excitement.

'Are you sure this is what you want?' he says. 'It's not a woman's drink.'

'It's what I drink. Where do you come from?'

'Brisbane.'

'Oh yes, so you said.'

'No I didn't. I hope you're not going to dawdle over that drink.'

She doesn't mind getting it over quickly either. 'Why don't you have a shower while I have this?' she suggests.

'I don't need a shower.'

'I'd prefer you to have one. I just had one.'

'Oh, come off it.'

She decides to use a bit of crude charm to get her way. 'I'll come and dry your back.'

He can't win, won't push it. 'Will you get your gear off too?'

'If you're in such a hurry, let's fix the business up now.'

'I'll fix it up later.'

'It's done before.'

'Don't you trust me? I'll pay after.'

'It's the rules and I keep them.'

'Come off it, you don't need rules with me.'

'I can't stay if we don't do it first.'

She wouldn't stay, and won't bother going on with this. She has put down her drink and sits alert, ready to get up and go. He relents, he doesn't want it to get too hostile.

'Jeez, you drive a hard bargain. All the same, you lot, tough as they make them.'

'Could be.' She is watching him, without expression.

He is going through his wallet. 'Do you take Diners?'

He is going through his wallet. 'Do you take cash?'

He thinks he's funny. She is watching him, without expression. He is young, a show-off, a real smartarse, a new breed of businessman: trendy, druggy, hard. His attitude to her is both respectful and disrespectful: respect for emotionless sex and for business and for illegality, disrespect for women in general. Bourbon and coke for him, no coke in hers. It's a self-contained unit of the type you rent by the week.

'Cash is fine.'

He counts out big notes and hands them to her, saying with approval, 'More than most people earn in a week there!' She refuses to respond to that and he says, 'How much does the boss get?'

'She gets her share.'

'How much is that? She probably gets half. No? She gets the booking fee and you get the rest?' Vita won't answer. 'Do you pay

19

much to get looked after?' Vita looks blank: what does he mean? 'Protection,' he says.

She smiles involuntarily; he is preposterous. 'Yeah, and I'm a helpless white slave and my life is full of crime and drugs and pimps and corruption!'

'Sounds all right to me!' And because he means it, she quite likes him. He is encouraged. 'You'd be mad to work straight, right. I've had to protect a few deals by fixing up the right people myself. Shows you what a lot of bloody fools there are out there, thinking it's just a matter of what you're told. You'd know that. I'll tell you something as a favour: if you were smart you'd be working for yourself, no paying out to the boss...'

He likes having some company. She is in a very relaxed posture, half-sitting, half-lying, on the sofa.

She is in a very relaxed posture, half-sitting, half-lying, on the bed. He likes having some company. He is a Japanese businessman. She reads what they've been writing on the hotel stationery: some Japanese words he's been teaching her—it's a way to have a conversation. The room is full of huge packages with Duty Free labels and cartons of Japanese cigarettes—an open pack is by the bed.

'Hi, how are you: *konichi wa*. Thank you: *arigato.* Goodbye: *sayonara. Ichi, ni, san, yon, go.* How's that?'

'Good, good,' he says. 'May I?' He moves to sit pressed up against her.

'You certainly may, why not, I guess it's time.'

'May I?' he says, as he reaches for her breasts. He pauses then. 'You married?'

'No.'

'No? No?'

'No.'

'May I?' Touching her. 'May I?' Reaching for her knickers, drawing them aside for a long, fascinated look. He is busy with her body. She is watching him, without expression.

*　　　*　　　*

20

She is watching him, without expression. He has finished with her body. He is a straight, middle-everything businessman, and, right now, very pleased with himself.

'And I thought I wouldn't make it.'

'I told you you'd have no trouble with me.'

'I don't know what it is usually.'

'It's your head.'

'All in the mind you reckon. Have you been doing this long?'

There is a champagne bottle in a bucket near the bed, glasses half full; a fancy room service tray of cellophane wrappings and ribbons and flowers and fancy edible fruit; empty oyster shells; leftover smoked salmon and other party food. His briefcase, folders of papers and printed reports sit on another table. She hasn't answered him.

'Can you stay for a while?' he asks.

She hasn't answered him. 'Can you stay for a while?' he asks again.

He has the largest suite in the hotel, and she'd been arranged by his assistants. She laughs. He had too much power at work. She'd had to boss him around, command him and reprimand him, before he'd relax. She'd even had to slap him, hard. Not something you'd plan on doing, but it was just the thing. Now he wants her to stay.

Now he wants her to stay.

Now he wants her to leave.

That's usually the way it goes.

7

The Sex Part

How could she do it? What if she didn't like him?

The unknown man. He puts his papers in a neat pile. He puts them in his briefcase. He has a shower and puts on a bathrobe. He has a shower and gets dressed again. He waits to have a shower with her. He doesn't think about a shower until she arrives. He thinks about a shower but does he want her to know he just came out of the shower? He has a shower and smears on the deodorant. He hopes she's a girl who appreciates personal freshness. He hopes she's as good as the last one. He hopes she's better than the last one. He doesn't think about it. He catches up on some phone calls while there's time. He has a drink. He orders champagne. He doesn't order yet, not until he has had a look at her. He remembers why he called. He hopes it'll be worth it. He doesn't care.

She knocks at the door. She's immediately at home, sitting at ease, kicking her shoes off, hoping he hasn't waited too long—it was hard to get a cab. She lets him notice her relief and pleasure that it's someone more attractive young distinguished or something more than she had dared to hope. She'd love a drink. Better get you-know-what out of the way, enjoy ourselves. Is it cash? He wants to know how much, how long, how good. He doesn't ask a thing. It's ready. It's in an envelope. He has to find his wallet. Is there any hurry?

He can see he has her attention. He has her interest. Interesting. Where does he live? Oh yes, so he said. Never been there, is it nice, interesting? He's looking at her. She's got nice tits. She's got tits. She's got nice legs. Those awful pantihose or real stockings? Suspenders, lace, black, red, flesh, silk, nylon? He wonders. He hopes. He doesn't care about these things. She's wearing pants. Casual, kinky. She's got personality. He likes the smile, a mind of her own. Smart. Professional. But not too blasé. Oops. He likes her passive, feminine, dumb, admiring. That's better. Has she been doing this long? Of course, it's relative. But he can tell it wouldn't be long—she's not hard. Don't get hard. That's right, he laughs—nervously, heartily, not at all—ladies shouldn't be hard. Men should be hard. A hard man is good to find. (A good man is harder.)

Another drink? Maybe later. After. Get comfortable now. Take off the tie for a start. How do you feel? It'll be good. He watches her undress. She loves it. Show-off. Nympho. Sex maniac. Bullshitter.

Her hands on her own breasts, her own thighs; her hips moving against the cold sheets; the cold sheets make her giggle. Come here, make me warm. Put your hands here. She replaces her hands with his over her cunningly hardened nipples. He lowers his face to hers. The big moment: does she kiss? She moves her head swiftly at the last second, bites his shoulder, leaving him thrusting his tongue at the air stupidly, like a fish. She's got a boyfriend, you can tell that if she doesn't kiss him. He doesn't think of kissing her. Kissing has no part in this. He doesn't want to kiss. He begs for a kiss. He won't ask again. He'd better not. She pushes his head to her breast. There, nice, like that, don't bite, careful, gently please, no teeth. He kisses her nipples. He sucks gently. He sucks hard. He's not into tits at all.

He hasn't got this far. He's sitting on the end of the bed. He has to tell her. He sometimes has a bit of trouble. It's all right, and she looks him in the eye, steady, confident, you won't have any trouble with me. She undoes the top button of his shirt. She pulls the shirt apart and presses her mouth to the bare triangle of flesh. Next button, her wet mouth sliding down. Next button. Her tongue flicking over his nipples. One side. The other side. Down to the belt. He takes it off, she can't. Good. Pushes him back, says don't do a thing. Her wet, sliding mouth on his bare stomach. Lifts the underpants, eases them over, aside. He's growing. He's hard and eager. He isn't yet. He soon is. Her hands underneath him, cupping, holding, stroking. Her hair on his stomach. Her tongue flicking, slurping, sliding. No trouble with

23

me. He's ready. A bit more. That'll do. She tugs at the pants. He takes them off. She rolls over on the bed. He's busy pulling his pants off his ankles. She quickly spits the gathered saliva onto her fingers and applies it. She is posed, classical, her hands pushing on her thighs. She's wide open. She glistens, she beckons, she flows. Come on, come on.

Oh God, he's the nouvelle cuisine type. He had minted eggplant puree for dinner, topped with pickled prawns in a marmalade glaze. He knows these days it's ladies first. Gentlemen come later. It's his turn for her turn. All right then. Good, don't bite, gently please, no teeth, no, there, like that. She's tensely ready to jerk his head off by the ears. She's never been so relaxed, sinking, flowing. She can't stand it any more. It's time for the killing to start. They should never have been told about the clitoris. Her most hated question, did you come? Oh God he's a talker. Tell me what you want. What do you want? Where will I put it? What am I doing? Tell me. Say it. Do you like it? Where is it? What is, what's in your cunt? Baby. Baby.

It wasn't like that. He had a plain steak for dinner. He grabbed her arse, got on top, said nothing, grunted once, it was over.

It wasn't like that. He's a stayer; an athlete. He turns her over; he's read magazines; he wants her on top; he turns her over and over again. He knows tricks, he can make her move, he can make her moan. Don't stop, she moans to him, don't stop. He has stopped. He's finished, she said the wrong thing. She listens. He moans, she sighs. He yells, she cries out. He doesn't make a sound, she's dead, slowly coming alive. She places her hands to check his heart. He's already quietly finished. He's just starting, building up speed, ready to pound furiously, announce his arrival; a fanfare. He takes her with him. He fills her. She's throbbing, streaming, clutching.

Are you wet? Are you hard? Can you feel it? Do you like it? What am I doing? Do you believe me? Do you want more?

24

Suppose there's more. He's well read, he knows things. He goes for the works. The endless falling into darkness, falling into his iron manly flesh, the hot kisses gulped like wine adding heat to her body, drinking deeply, the sucking mouth melting into mouth, seeking the leaping tongues, the eyes alight, the febrile waves trembling there, the pools of madness, the exquisite torment, her hair damp as seaweed, her taste like a seashell like a camellia like a rose, the velvet the silky, salty flesh; tigerlike he's tearing open the fur, the frenzy, the steaming tides, the hot springs, the wound of ecstasy which rents her body like lightning, the beatitudes, the tightness like a sheath closed over him softly caressing, gripping, the sweet insistent stabbing, her back arching to meet his thrusting, the flicking darts of fire, the molten languor spreading through her body.

It wasn't like that. He rolls over silently and turns his back to her. He rolls over and lights a cigarette. He holds her as if it should never end. He asks about her boyfriend, children, interests. He pays for another hour. He says she can go. He wonders why he does this. He feels gratified. He doesn't think. She has a shower, careful not to get her hair wet, drying herself hurriedly (or slowly) she looks at his after-shave, his pills, his toothbrush. It's a night to remember. They never think of each other again.

There's something about it that's rather like the real thing.

8

A Duck feather

Maybe every human encounter leaves behind its question marks; all of Violet's certainly did.

This particular question mark began with a phone call. (They all begin with a phone call.) It was Saturday night, about nine o'clock; a new client, a private address.

Violet was prepared: she'd find another version of a familiar scene—another new flat, newly furnished for another new life; a new divorce leaving another man newly incapable of spending an evening alone. His mates from work would be tied up with their families on the weekend. There'd be nothing worth watching on the television and after a couple of drinks he'd get to thinking about his kids...

But this night the door was opened by a tall, dark boy—thin, pale, nervous. His voice was gentle, he was dressed in soft cotton drawstring pants, a white silk shirt. The lighting was subdued, the radio was on a classical music station.

He apologised for not having chairs; he supposed Violet was not used to sitting on floors.

'No I'm not but I like it,' she said, choosing some batik-covered cushions from the pile on the white Moroccan carpet. 'This is nice,' she said. It was nice. Violet had never sat on floors. Vita did that.

There were large, illustrated books and sketch pads lying around—he had obviously just been doing some drawing. She tried to see—birds, faces, ornate shapes, the words of a song: 'Here's to you Mrs Robinson Jesus loves you more than you will know, woe woe woe.' Woe indeed.

He watched her, seemed wary at first. She was unsure. She moved to affect a new personality to match his unaffected air of delicacy. He relaxed a little while she admired a cloth on the table; its colours were rich and warm.

'Is this from Indonesia? Have you been there?'

He watched her closely as she looked at it and talked.

He had never called an escort agency before. He admitted this was the first time.

'Why tonight?' she asked.

'I felt lonely,' he said simply.

'Why did you choose Pamela's?'

He quite liked the advertisements. There was an open newspaper by the telephone.

'And,' he said, 'it's Saturday night.'

Oh yes, Saturday night. Everybody loves Saturday night. On Saturday night all girls are Asked Out and all boys have Dates and everyone has Parties and goes to the Movies and Drinks Too Much and Falls In Love and Dances All Night, and everyone has Someone on Saturday Night and no-one Sleeps Alone.

'It's a good night to stay at home,' Violet said. '. . . Especially here,' she added. It was a nice place. 'Well,' she said, 'this is how it's done, first we get business out of the way. . .'

'Yes, of course. She said fifty dollars. Is that right?'

'Ah. The fifty dollars is a booking fee only. . .'

'What does that mean?'

'That covers only "the young lady's company on a social basis". Didn't she say all that?'

'I hoped. . . I wanted more.' It was difficult for him.

'Yes. Then you offer me more money. I do not solicit it. More starts at a hundred dollars, I'm afraid. Let's say a hundred dollars extra.' Just for him.

He went out of the room and came back with cash.

'How long will you stay?'

If he had asked Pamela he would have been told, 'that is between you and the young lady'. The girl had to try to leave sooner, the man to keep her longer. That was one of the games.

'I'll stay a while,' said Violet. 'I'm not looking at the clock; I won't rush off.'

27

He sat down. Self-mockingly he asked her what happened next.

'Well,' she said, 'it would be very nice if you were to offer me a drink.'

He didn't drink. He didn't have any liquor in the flat. He was diabetic and not allowed to drink. Oh yes, but there was *something*. He went out to the refrigerator and brought back a bottle of Veuve Cliquot. Violet approved. People who aren't allowed to drink should drink champagne. They drank the bottle while he showed her some of his Asian cloths and carvings.

Violet was not what he expected. He had been apprehensive. He admitted regretting his call. Thought he might get a tough, unsympathetic old tart no doubt, although he did not say so.

'But you came,' he said, smiling at her.

'You aren't what I expected either,' she said. He asked her what kind of people she usually met and she told him.

Did they ask her very much about herself, he wondered. No, they didn't.

'What do they ask you?'

'Nothing very personal,' she told him, 'unless they're after a tragic tale of my "slide into sin".'

' "What's a nice girl like you..." '

'Yes. Questions like that.'

In his bedroom there were more of the richly coloured fabrics, books, drawings. 'A brief affair,' he said, as they moved towards the bed. An affair? thought Violet. He had printed sheets.

'Afterwards', as they say, he brought her coffee and then she had to leave. He asked her to stay. She couldn't possibly, she insisted, and made him call a taxi while she dressed. He wanted to give her something, a present.

'Do you collect anything?'

'I collect ducks,' Violet said.

He took a feather from a vase filled with feathers. 'It's a duck feather,' he said. 'I don't have any ducks.'

'It's beautiful. It's not from a drake by any chance?'

'Let's look it up.' He took one of the large, illustrated volumes. 'What's that—*What Feather is That*?'

They found it in the book of birds, and even a picture of the duck. Then she ran out to get her taxi. There was a commotion below, a fight in the street. A loud party in the opposite building was spreading onto the pavement. Taxis drew up and pulled away filled with yahooing partygoers.

She turned, he was at his window; she blew a kiss.

'Violet,' he called.

She walked back a bit. 'I think they took my taxi,' she called up to him. 'Would you ring again?'

'Do you want to wait up here?'

She went back into the building, back into his flat, and stayed the night. 'I know exactly why a nice girl like you is doing a job like this,' he said.

They sat up in bed and watched the late movies. He did that a lot. It was the part of television she liked best. They drank tea. There was no more champagne.

'This colour here,' he pointed, 'is violet, isn't it?' She did not answer. Sweet but pathetic, she thought. Different but the same.

She woke up early, suddenly, crept out of bed and began to dress.

'Violet,' he said, 'you haven't slept enough.'

'Maybe not. But I'm going now.'

She was sure he would be at the window again. The taxi came. She did not look up. Violet's existence could not include cosy companionable Sunday mornings. They weren't paid for.

9

As for Vita's Existence

She would say that her life had improved, free of the cycle of unemployment and more or less boring jobs. 'What's the use of an education if you can't spend it?' she'd say, paying the bill. The modern woman was supposed to struggle eternally with the conflicting calls of career and marriage ('partnership' for the fashionable) yet Vita found herself uncalled by anything but the desire to live a day-to-day hedonism. She spent big.

Girls have girlfriends. Girlfriends are part of the best in life—they know what's important and don't leave you wondering what they really meant. Spending time with Catherine were the moments Vita most adored. Catherine and Vita would go out to lunch, to a film, or shopping. They loved hearing each other's observations. Vita thought Catherine's were hilarious. They would note each other's unspoken reactions and laugh at things no-one else saw. It was love. On some evenings Catherine would visit Vita in her city flat, with its clutter, its lack of cohesion or pattern—except for the ducks on the wall—giving the impression of objects acquired with a changeable sense of direction. Girlfriends talk about everything and don't leave out talking about men.

Catherine had been called from both sides: career and marriage. She had answered and struggled and lost. Vita's sense of remoteness from such choices was encouraged by Catherine's comically dismal accounts of life as a serious career woman and wife. Catherine, these days, liked to share in the sense of remoteness.

It seemed to bring out the voyeur in people when Vita discussed her job. It didn't feel like exhibitionism: she was another voyeur, watching and examining Violet's life; quite detached from it. Violet's life was full of men. Catherine and Vita had men in their lives, too.

30

'We do know some men at least,' said Vita. 'Lots of fun and dates with witty, attractive men who can dance and be funny. Then, at the end of the night, the boys go home together and the girls think being a fag-hag has its lonely side.'

'Although,' Catherine said, 'it has its positive side when you look at the alternative. What kind of tea are you making?'

'Do you want herbal or ordinary? What alternative? The new kind of man? The gentle, feminist kind of man?'

'Well, you do wonder, don't you?' said Catherine, with an unaffected sigh. 'Men are supposed to be changing, but into *what*?'

'The liberated kind are worse,' said Vita. 'They're into being very aware but they think being aware of the clitoris is more important than being aware of champagne.'

'I'm not actually fond of champagne, as a drink,' said Catherine, 'but you can't beat it as a gesture. Where are the old-fashioned men who order champagne?'

Vita poured the tea. 'Ordering girls along with the champagne on the expense account,' she said, with an exaggerated self-satisfied gaiety. Catherine looked at her soberly and Vita knew she would be constantly scrutinised for a sign that it was Getting To Her.

'Yes,' said Catherine. 'But it must be unpleasant sometimes. Someone really ugly, unbearable.'

'Oh, after a while,' said Vita, 'she said with a world-weary air, it makes no difference. As they say: a cigar is a cigar...'

'Do you ever see any of them again?' Catherine asked.

'Give me time!' The phone rang. Vita went to answer, but hesitated. 'The idea is to make them want to come back,' she said. 'If someone wants to see you again you can make him give you more things. Dollars, preferably. Then they're called "regulars".' They both thought that was funny.

It was Pamela on the phone, with a job. Someone who would turn out to be a regular.

'He's a bit difficult, I'm afraid,' Pamela said, 'but he always pays well. He wants someone who can talk about art.' So she picked Violet.

'My God! Imagine,' Vita said to Catherine, 'I've got to go and meet someone who wants to talk about "art".' She got out her make-up.

'Paintings? Or as in Larger than Life?'

'We shall see.' Then, being practical, she asked, 'Can I get away with this outfit? Sure!' she answered herself.

'Do you often have to talk about "art"?' Catherine asked, taking the cups to the kitchen.

'Never,' said Vita. 'Violet's the arty one.'

10

Violet Confesses

My first impression of Len Bloom was one of damp nervousness, and it was every impression thereafter.

'What do you drink?' he asked. At least he asked.

'Whisky.'

'Whisky Sour?'

'What's that?' I acted dumb. I didn't want port again.

'They make a very good Whisky Sour here.' He ordered two from room service.

'Mmm, delicious,' I said. I drank it quickly and ate the cherry. He ordered four more.

After that we always drank Whisky Sours, even through the room service dinners. Cocktails went well with them. A tray of Whisky Sours would always be waiting when I arrived and then Bloom would have his little joke: he would give me fifty dollars.

'Come on, Bloom,' I'd say, 'I'm not here just to talk to you.' I always pretended that we fucked. He gave me more money. 'Well then, I might stay a little longer,' I'd say. He gave me more. 'Stay the night,' he would say. 'Lucky for you I'm made of money.' Lucky for me I needed more.

He came to Sydney on business meetings. His business seemed to be owning things. The next day would begin with a business meeting over breakfast—after I'd left, of course.

He would always want me to stay the night. He would talk and talk. After dinner we would undress and talk in bed, or rather *he* would talk. My replies would become shorter and shorter till my final grunts. If I managed to fall asleep for a while, he'd wake me, and I'd find him sitting up, drinking from a bottle of Scotch. He'd have thrown off the bedcovers; he was always hot and damp.

'Don't you ever sleep?' I'd ask, drawing the blankets back over me.

'Oh yes,' he'd say. 'I have some very good sleeping pills but they're not working tonight.' His pills never worked.

I never found out what Bloom meant by Art. He never mentioned plays, films or concerts. He didn't collect paintings. He did read.

He was reading *Papillon* when I first met him, and listening to a tape of an Irish actor reading *The Ballad of Reading Gaol*. Bloom was very fond of him, of his mellifluous voice. Maybe that was the Art. During my first evening with him, I had to listen to it all the way through.

'I hate that kind of delivery,' I said. 'If a poem is good you want to listen to it and not to vocal callisthenics, and if it's no good you can't make it good by madly putting expression into it.'

Why was Violet sounding like this? I was drunk. Something about deflated, humid Bloom provoked a sly aggression. But as I became more contrary, he became more fond. When he decided that I loved reading as much as he did, he was delighted. This avoided the subject of my personal history.

'We could read the same books,' he suggested, sweating profusely, 'and talk about them when we meet.' I smiled, though it was an effort. He once had a mistress who read the same books as him and the two of them would take a motel room and discuss the books in bed. Also, she had multiple orgasms and was his best friend.

'Tell me, Violet, do you have multiple orgasms?'

'Not me, one orgasm and I've had it.'

When his wife found out about the mistress, he'd had to choose and never saw the mistress again. The lot of them had then started to go to psychoanalysts and encounter groups.

'Why did you have to choose?' I asked. 'Why did you choose your wife?'

He explained: he hadn't wanted to choose, but his wife didn't believe in Open Marriage. Bloom had wanted her to read a book on Open Marriage but she refused. Now he wanted me to read

34

it. I said I had already heard about it. The ex-mistress's husband had not believed in Open Marriage either. Bloom was much impressed with the idea that people could have a Relationship without Being Possessive.

It was as much as I could bear. Businessmen usually had a straightforward double standard and had not heard of encounter groups. I was beginning to think it was just as well.

'I'm not interested in any kind of relationship or marriage,' I said, 'and I don't go in for any kind of morality, new or otherwise.'

Had I gone too far? Why couldn't I just congratulate him on his broadmindedness? And I had spoken crossly. It was a long night—him sweating and stammering, labouring away at these ideas. It would have been easier if there had been sex. Bloom wanted to share his thoughts. I might have relented, but when I didn't, he was all the more intrigued and insisted on knowing my Views.

I knew what he was after. I was exactly what he had in mind to replace his mistress. He wanted my private telephone number. He wanted me to trust him. He believed we were on the same side in the sexual revolution he'd heard about. He thought it was a good idea to get what you wanted. He didn't know it was another way to kill the thing you love.

He said, 'I bought a gold mine today, so you'd better be nice to me.'

'I don't have to be nice to you.'

'Have I told you about my opal mine? I've got some beautiful opals...'

'I don't like opals. I do like gold. I love gold; gold makes me happy.'

I think he told me some things about 'business'. He hinted that buying and selling mines was not simple. Staying awake drinking whisky all night must have helped him make all these important decisions. Or maybe it was the pills he took in the morning.

'What are these?' I pointed to one of several packets.

'Anti-depressants.'

I asked to try one—I was never depressed, I just wanted to see what would happen.

He tried to show me the documents in his case. These, he claimed, would prove he was wealthy, and successful in business. As if his interest in Art might cause doubt.

I wouldn't look at them. 'I don't understand stuff like that,' I said. 'I don't care if you don't really own a gold mine.'

'I'd like to bring you a present.'

'A diamond bracelet would be nice.'

'I haven't known you long enough for that,' he said, without humour. 'I will look for a token of my esteem.' He started saying I'd never have to work again, that he'd look after me. I got very cross. Maybe fair exchange is priceless.

He could have afforded the diamond bracelet and it would have been proof that these charades could be put down to expenses. He gave me a large parcel and a note: 'Here are some books on travel which I chose myself because you want to travel. Love, LB.'

I got it: he had a problem with values.

I put the parcel on the floor under the back seat of the taxi and left it there.

Soon after that Violet was no longer to be found. There is no chronology in my sordid history.

11
Getting Started

Vita grew more certain that accounts of her lousy childhood, alienating jobs, treacherous lovers, lifestyle experiments and disillusionments were mere complications and explained nothing about Violet's existence at all. Nor did the hindsight of her growing conviction that we all invent ourselves. That didn't explain anything either. So how did a nice girl get started? Typically, she had a friend who tried it first.

'I'm trying to break into crime,' Vita said at a party. 'Fun and wealth is what I'm after.'

'You should talk to Liz Doran,' her friends said. 'She's got an interesting new job.'

The party was in a collective art studio that produced posters for radical causes. When you came in you paid a dollar and got a stamp on your hand. Ideological soundness was displayed by allegiance to The Look: mid-'seventies drab, i.e. post-'sixties, pre-punk. Women had very short haircuts, rolled up overalls and long, striped socks; T-shirts had slogans emblazoned on the front: 'Unbashed poofter', 'How dare you presume I'm a natural redhead', and 'Legalise it'; and tapes were played while the new-wave-ish rock-revival band got into the mood.

Vita wore overalls too, but they were floral silk—typical of her unsound individualism.

One of her friends pulled out an object that the others had seen before, and they fell about cackling. It was a gaudy bit of pink and green nylon frill. Vita held her hand out to examine this curiosity and couldn't make it out. What were all the pieces for? Robbo explained its function (it was a pair of crutchless knickers) by holding it up against her overalls: an image so ludicrous it was beyond offensiveness. Susan explained that it was a good-luck present for Liz.

Liz had a degree in medicine but she didn't practise. She spent a lot of time campaigning against the medical profession, studying herbalism and witchcraft, writing a Be Your Own Doctor kind of publication with a bickering female collective, dashing back and forth from various country areas where you went to get your head together (as some still put it), and getting into debt. She made a regular hyperactive seem as calm as Buddha. Her financial and personal affairs were a labyrinth of complications. A few weeks after the party, Liz killed herself by driving her car off a cliff in Queensland. She hadn't had any sleep for two days.

Their mutual friends at the party told Vita that Liz was working for an 'escort agency'—an appellation that sounded so ridiculous they all fell about laughing. Away from such a world, the idea of swapping money for company seemed preposterous and unreal.

Later that evening, Vita stepped outside and joined a group that was taking some air, talking, smoking joints, passing a can of beer around. The mood was later-in-the-evening intense. Ruth was saying, 'Liz cannot possibly believe you can fool around with the sexual proclivities of men and not get hurt. Middle-class women *trying* prostitution! How dare they!'

'I saw you talking to Liz,' said Mara. 'Are you going to do it?'

'Why not?' said Vita. 'See what it's like, anyway. I mean, you don't sign any contract.'

'You've got to be kidding, Vita. There's no way Liz is going through with it. Rape is not a joke.'

'What rape? If you're getting paid it's not rape—unless the cheque bounces,' said Vita, unfortunately.

Ruth was furious and disgusted; this was something she felt really passionate about. 'Liz is off the air for even considering it. She's a feminist. What kind of support is that for women who are trying to escape *real* oppression? And I don't mean some bourgeois search for individuality.'

'Look, if you're going to fuck men,' said Mara, 'and Christ knows why anyone would, you might as well get as much as you can from them.'

'It's just not on,' argued her friend. 'No way. The real world is a vicious place and you don't have any control over that.'

'If you think the world is vicious,' Vita said, 'you'll find it is vicious. But I don't.'

'Look,' began the group's diplomat, 'feminism, understandably, can get entangled with moralism...'

Ruth exploded. 'You fucking anarchists are more concerned with moralism than with the *facts* of male oppression...'

'Oh, thisism and thatism,' said Vita, softly, leaving the argument. 'I heard that all isms are now wasms.'

So Vita rang the number Liz had given her, a number where Liz was known as Jill. Pamela invited Vita to come over. Her office, the front room of a smart little house close to the city, had a look of desperate expensiveness. There was her huge desk; a couple of sofas, rugs, drooping potplants; a tiger skin; magazines on the coffee table; lurid oil painting of a nude; and, on the desk, a framed slogan: 'Life is like a shit sandwich; the more bread you have, the less shit you eat'.

Pamela was glaringly well groomed, conservatively and expensively dressed. She was a rich woman, who had not been brought up with money but had made a conscious effort to acquire the manners of wealth and taste from magazines and from the men she had met when she, herself, was a call-girl, back in those better days.

Pamela's cool gaze betrayed a cool-gaze act. Pamela told Vita that the girls who did well with her were usually a certain type: a bit of an ego-tripper, a bit of an actress, and the kind of girl who liked the best things in life without having been provided for. She said she had her rules, and so on.

Vita gave it a go. She became Violet.

'Do you think you can handle it?' Pamela asked.

'Oh yes,' said Violet, and started that night.

She came back when she had to, to settle the accounts. 'So that works out as...' Pamela would say. 'I owe you $200 cash. Is that

39

what you make it? Good, I'm glad you can fill out the forms all right. Sometimes you get a new girl you think'll be okay and then you find she can never fill out a Bankcard the right way.'

'Only,' said Vita, 'I never know if I should put "goods" or "services".'

Pamela quite appreciated that. 'You ought to get yourself a beeper,' she said. She opened a drawer and took out an electronic paging device. She dialled a number on her phone as she explained, 'You can go out and I can call you wherever you are. You can go to the pictures or to the Hilton.'

'You can always tell people you're a nurse or something,' offered Susie, who had come in during the conversation. Susie was a cute, blonde, brash, bosomy, twenty-two-year-old, who had found her vocation in the *Playboy* Bunny image—an image she believed in with all her heart.

The little device began its shrill beeping. Pamela said, 'There's a model that vibrates instead of beeping, so no-one has to know.'

'Great. Could wear it in my pants,' Vita muttered, so they could ignore it, and they did.

'I can get a good price on them.'

'Oh, I'm happy staying at home till you ring.'

'Couldn't you kick yourself,' said Susie, as a welcome to Vita, 'all those years you were giving it away!' She was there with her girlfriend Faye: a slightly older, exotic looking, fringe-dweller type. Faye had an intensity without vitality, and usually looked spaced out—despite the carefully applied heavy make-up she always wore.

'Susie's got a regular who's already taken her to Hawaii, first class,' said Pamela. 'She got a nice ring, too.'

'He phoned me up last night and said he was thinking of leaving his wife!' Susie said immodestly.

'I've heard that one before,' said Pamela. 'Give them your phone number and soon they expect you to come round for nothing. And no giving *your* number to clients!' she said to Vita. 'I find out about that and you're out!'

That night there was a double booking and Pamela said to come over to the office to meet the other girl and they could go together. It was Liz. They screamed happily and hugged each other.

'I knew Jill before,' Violet reminded Pamela. 'She gave me your number.'

'Oh yes,' Pamela answered, cool as always, considering them. 'I'm glad you two get on so well, but don't let the men feel left out. Off you go; don't be late. Have a nice time.'

Liz had her car.

'Well, my dear, what about all this? What do you think?'

'Vita, this is the best thing I've ever done. I think Pamela is terrific,' Liz said.

'*Do* you? Listen, she really impressed me, so tough, no bullshit. Yet this business is meant to be so—what would they say. . .'

'The worst exploitation of women, the most sexist. . . I can tell you I've never felt *less* exploited in a job. And the women in it really know how to make the best life for themselves. Have you met Amber, or Ellie? They're so strong and independent, without education or the women's movement or anything.' Prostitution was no challenge to Liz's idealism. 'Could you just fuck anyone casually again? I couldn't, now I know what I'm worth.'

They parked at the hotel. 'Come on, Jill,' Vita said, preening, 'our blind dates are waiting. Just be nice to the gentlemen, Fancy, and they'll be nice to you.'

'Violet—was that your grandmother's name or something?'

'No, I just made it up.'

12

Getting Tough

The blind dates had a suite, a tape recorder playing loudly, champagne in buckets. They intended to party, greeted the girls enthusiastically, ordered more champagne, turned up the music, asked them to dance. Soon the room was littered with empty bottles.

They were youngish South Africans. In a moment of masculine seriousness they hinted at some important business: a rendezvous at the embassy the next day. Showing off. They believed that women impressed with importance give more of themselves.

All four drank a lot. The girls did hilarious stripteases on the table. More champagne arrived. They squirted it over each other and threw it about. A chair was overturned, bottles smashed. They pissed themselves laughing. The phone rang, they were asked to turn down the noise. Turn down the noise was the funniest thing they'd ever heard. The phone rang again.

Then two of them were in the bath. Liz and her companion pranced in naked, clutching each other and giggling. She had a hat on and his socks and he had something draped around his neck. The bath was full, foaming with several packets of bubble bath. They threw some more champagne over Vita and the other man and pranced out again. Violet blew foam around the bathroom. There was silence, the tape ended and stayed off.

Violet realised they'd stopped laughing. The mood had become sombre. 'Violet, Violet,' he was saying, clutching at her in the slippery bath. How he had wanted to meet someone like her. He had been waiting for her. On he went, urgent in drunken sentiment.

She was new to the role and this was the first time she had met a man who had ordered a whore but then revealed he had been asking for true love.

'Don't say that,' she said. 'Stop it,' she wept.

'I love you,' he insisted.

'Stop it,' she sobbed. 'You're not supposed to say that.' It was a drunken hysteria.

'Why not—Violet, I love you. Why did we have to meet this way?'

She did not find that at all funny. 'You don't know what you're saying,' she said. 'This is all make-believe. There's no such person as me.'

Then he told her to get dressed, go out and come back in. He wanted her to come back to show him she chose to be with him, to make love with him because she wanted to. 'Of your own free will,' he put it.

He kept begging; he began crying. He *needed* her to choose him. 'Just stop it,' she said, crossly now. 'Don't pretend. If I go I won't come back.'

Somehow, it seemed the next minute, they were suddenly lying together on the sofa. Liz and the other man had evidently gone into the bedroom. Violet and whatsisname were covered by a blanket and he had just silently fucked her. They were lying there quietly when Liz came out of the other room. Vita got up, collected her clothes and went into the flooded and messed up bathroom. The girls dressed quickly; they were pale and serious.

They went back into the room. The men were both sitting on the sofa, wearing bathrobes.

Liz asked for the money. Her client said something like, 'what money?' and stared at her insolently. The other man looked away and kept silent and as long as the girls remained, he did not look their way nor utter a word.

Liz was brisk, firm. 'You made a booking with our agency and the terms were agreed upon. I was told you were using an American Express card. We've spent many hours with you, had a good time with you and fucked you. Now we're going. Give me your card so I can fill in the rest of the form, you sign it and we'll go.'

'What's this for?' he said, looking at what she'd already written there.

'That is the booking fee plus the extra costs, as you already know.'

'Do you really think,' he said, 'that you're worth that much?'

Vita was dumbfounded.

'How much do you think it's worth,' Liz asked coldly, 'to get up in the middle of the night, make sure you look your best, go and meet someone you've never seen, be nice to him, and fuck him whether you feel like it or not? How much would you charge to do that?'

They argued for a while. He seemed adamant he wasn't going to sign it.

'I'll call the police,' he said.

Vita sat, silently panicking. 'Please do,' said Liz, unruffled. 'Go ahead.'

He went to the telephone and dialled. Then he hung up but stayed by the phone. 'You wouldn't want me to call the police. You'll get into trouble.' Until then Vita hadn't known he was bluffing.

At last he went to his wallet and took out his credit card. Liz copied his details and handed him the form. Before he signed, the other one rose suddenly, snatched the form, tore it up and went into the bedroom, out of sight. Liz calmly took another form and repeated the procedure.

At last they were driving out of the hotel.

'God, we're amateurs,' said Liz. 'I wouldn't have been able to face Pamela if we hadn't got it.'

'It's incredible. How can people be so awful—after all that laughing and dancing.' Misery, then nausea. 'Stop, I'm going to be sick.'

'No you're not,' Liz said firmly. 'And stop performing. So, they weren't exactly the nicest people we've ever met.'

Vita understood. It was part of the deal. You had no time to waste in minding. You learnt; you got tough; it never happened again.

Liz dropped her home. 'No drinking like that again! Money first!'

'Okay.' They looked at each other and managed a small laugh. Then Liz drove off, leaving her. In the faintest first light of day she turned thankfully to her soothing shower, her favourite record, the old silk shirt she slept in, her own calm bed.

13

No Difference After All

The phone must have rung for minutes before Vita could drag her mind into consciousness. She had to go and meet Pamela and her lawyer straight away. Her head felt like lead—it must have been all those pills. She could sleep for another week.

'Cold shower, coffee, get moving, get it over,' she muttered, trying to hasten into her more usual rhythm. 'This'll be dreadful. It's ten o'clock; by noon it'll all be over.'

The lawyer was drinking tea with Pamela in her office.

'This is Charlie,' said Pamela. He was florid, hearty. 'Charlie, this is Violet.'

'I've heard people promise they'll fuck you to death,' he guffawed in greeting, 'but this is the first time I've known someone to do it.' Violet sat down. 'What a way to go, eh?' he sighed, in great amusement.

'Will you have some tea?' Pamela offered.

'Oh please, I'm so dehydrated.'

'You'd better tell Charlie what was in the statement you made to the cops,' Pamela said.

Why did Violet have to tell him? Pamela had been there, she could have told him.

The cops had arrived about an hour after Violet had been brought back to the office the night before. Pamela had given her a brandy and two more Valium and told her what she should tell the police. When they arrived, Violet had been lying not awake not asleep not dreaming not thinking. Dreadful words struggled into her apprehension. Inquest. Court. Coroner. Cross-examination. Press.

Violet knew what she might say and what she must not say. There was an odd legal situation, so that in the statement she had to claim she had received only the booking fee. Performing introductions for a fee was not illegal.

'You didn't have sex with him?' repeated the cop who was doing all the talking. That was how fucking was referred to by the law, which, in this matter, respected euphemism more than precision. He had removed his cap and jacket and had sat down to write. His younger offsider had evidently been given a non-speaking part. He stood in full uniform, wordless throughout. 'You'd better tell me if you did. It'll show up on the postmortem anyway.'

She shook her head. No sex.

'Did he, uh, get aroused?' the cop asked. He was only doing his job.

'Ah well, he was being sort of suggestive.' She blushed. She had to tell these lies, no-one wanted any extra trouble.

'You know how men are,' Pamela said silkily. 'A man will inevitably get aroused when alone with a young lady.'

'His clothes were in a pile in the room he was found in.' The cop was looking at his notes.

'He only had a dressing gown on when I arrived,' Violet obliged. 'I don't know why. Yes, I think I noticed the clothes. I don't know.' As instructed, she refused to sign the statement until she talked to the lawyer. Then the cops left and she was able to go, too. Pamela would ring as soon as she could get her lawyer over in the morning.

She told Charlie what she had been asked and what she had answered. 'And the difference between that and the truth is that I had accepted extra money and he was dressed when I arrived— oh, I suppose you don't have to know that.' She looked at Pamela who nodded at her to go on. 'I don't know what to tell you. He was impotent,' she said, listening to her own cracked voice: distant, flat, precise, 'but it seemed that he ejaculated at the moment of death.'

'I think that's normal, but I'll check. Good girl.'

'Well if that's all...' Violet stood.

It was all.

'You'll be on tonight,' Pamela said. Like getting straight back onto a horse after having a fall. 'Go and have a nice day. Go to a movie.'

She stumbled into a taxi where at last she surrendered to tears.

'He's not worth it, nice-looking girl, plenty more.' The driver cheered, feebly.

She hoped she'd heard the last of it. When the day was over she'd never think about it again. If she remembered it carefully one last time she could forget it. Only last night...

It had been a local booking; the house sat smugly in its sedate leafy street: an ordered and spacious suburb.

Her blind date was a man long past the middle age, short and stout with large, watery, blue eyes.

'I'm Violet.'

'I know, I know.' He beamed at her and showed her in. 'I am very pleased with you.' He had a pronounced Eastern European accent. Inside: polished floors, polished furniture, a few embroideries and objects 'from the homeland', great neatness. His wife was at a bridge party. She went out a lot. He was retired. His wife was not interested in sex any more. He didn't mind, very often, but sometimes he could not help it, he thought about a young girl, he got so excited, as he had that day, waiting for his wife to leave, and then he would telephone for someone. Unfortunately, last time the girl was skinny and too tall, but this time he was very pleased.

He quickly showed her around the house, except for the marital chamber whose door remained shut. He asked her to sit in his private room: a study with books and photographs and a single bed. She asked for a drink. He made some good, strong espresso, apologising for not having the Nescafé he knew Australians preferred. He put a record of Strauss waltzes on the player and watched her drink. At the last sip he threw off the bed cover, to the final sways of a Strauss waltz.

He tried and tried. That day he had been so excited, so hard, he repeated insistently. He pulled at himself, he clutched

48

at her, he pulled at her breasts, he strained and groaned and sweated.

'It doesn't matter,' Violet said. The hell it didn't. It mattered a lot to him. He was not interested in her consoling theories of love-making without penetration. He yanked at his cock—he would not let her touch it—and bashed at her body. He ground his flabby genitals into her thighs, panting, reddening, sweating in fury. He refused to begin slowly, to relax.

She became quietly furious also. Silly old goose. She gave up attempts either to arouse or console. Violet's usual obliging sweetness abated; she only endured the pitiful strivings of the creature labouring over her. At last he stopped; defeated.

He waddled out of the room and returned, dressed in a short dressing gown and slippers and carrying a large towel for her. He became a fond old man again. Would the beautiful young lady like some more coffee? She would like a drink of water. He poured some from a bottle, carefully washed the coffee cups and put them away.

In the living room she admired the embroideries and pointed to the piano.

'Do you play?' she asked, sweet eagerness again.

He did. She would love to hear him play. He had written a song, a song about his homeland, a prayer that one day she would again be free. He played the melody. He was going to play it at the wedding of a friend's daughter next week. They were going to have a traditional wedding, the groom was also a countryman, and there would be special prayers for their country and the choir would sing his song. He played it again.

Violet listened and watched, wrapped only in the towel. Then she asked to have a shower. Soon she would be able to go.

In the shower she remembered she still had her period. She squatted and removed the sponge. Standing, she squeezed it out under the warm jet. She had not realised that the blood would spray in all directions. Watery menstrual fluid splashed onto the shower curtain, the tiled wall, her body, and ran in pink swirls towards the drain. She hurriedly threw water at the spattered wall, finished rinsing the sponge and replaced it; washed away every last drop of the tainted rivulets. She trembled a bit. He might have come in. . . it was creepy.

The waltzes began again in the living room. He came in to watch her dry herself and followed her into his little room, where she began to dress. Suddenly he became frantic. She was going and he had not achieved erection, penetration. All day he had waited. Well, Violet had done what she could and the two hours were nearly over. He pleaded, then became angry. He mentioned the money he had paid; it made her icier. He pushed her a little and she lost her balance and sat on the bed. She was dressed, except for her shoes. She looked at him. It meant so much to him. He was sure he would make it. Good, then it wouldn't take long and he'd be happy and she could leave peacefully.

She removed only her skirt and pants, leaving on her bra and top. She lay on the bed and he stood at its foot. All right, she thought, any way you like. He left on his dressing gown, and began again to groan to strive to beat at his cock to push against her furiously. He would not listen. Again, he got redder in the face and sweat poured from his brow. Then he fell to the floor.

In one long, resounding heartbeat she realised he was quite still, quite silent.

She crouched by him. 'Are you all right?' she asked, stupidly. 'Oh, be all right,' she moaned. She shook him gently, then harder. 'Have life,' she pleaded. 'Have life have life.' In her last rational moment she grabbed the phone—right there by the bed—and dialled.

'Pamela, help, this old man here. . . he's had a heart attack I think. Help, please come here.' Her voice was rising and she slammed the receiver down. She tried desperately to remember how you gave artificial respiration. She straightened his body. Grim irony: from the limp cock trailed a creamy dribble. . .you breathed into the mouth holding the nose didn't you and then you forced the breath out by pressing your hands on his chest. Oh, God, no. The breath she had forced in, heated with prayer, returned as a wet gurgle. His face was blue.

She replaced her clothes. The distant Strauss soundtrack had stopped just then, or was it ages ago?

She heard people arrive, a female voice call her. In walked the apparitions of Amber and Susie in their evening finery. They had been at the office when she'd rung. Amber sat comforting her while Susie showed in the two ambulance men. She sat unmoving until the men came back into the room.

Violet stood. The one in front shook his head. 'We did everything we could . . .' She realised. She fainted.

'I've never fainted,' said Susie, on the way back to the office. 'What's it like?'

'Great' said Violet, and giggled. 'What was that you gave me?'

'Valium. Here, take some with you for later. I'm glad you're all right now. You know, I nearly got that job, but the old bloke didn't want anyone tall.' They agreed it was funny.

'We couldn't help laughing on the way over. Amber kept saying, "I hope she got the money first!" What a way to go! I said you'd get a reputation . . .'

'You poor darling,' Pamela said when they arrived. 'Why you, of all people . . . Have you got some Valium?' She gave Violet a couple.

The policemen who'd arrived later had said finally that they didn't think there'd be any trouble, the old bloke had a son who sounded a reasonable kind of fellow and who would be able to discourage his mother from inquiring further. And that was the end.

Vita left the taxi, darted through the harsh daylight to her darkened apartment and the soothing embrace of a long sleep. It was nearly noon; it was all over; the whole episode was a distant receding sound and fury. She would sleep and dream and forget and wake up clear and calm and life would go on as always.

14

All the Answers

Catherine had dropped over to see Vita after lunch.

'I told David that I thought being a poofter was silly,' she said. 'I said it was just a silly habit men get into. I thought he might be ready to cross the floor—over to me of course.' Catherine lit her cigarette. 'I sometimes see us with the three little ones, fruit of our passion kind of thing, though I haven't worked out in the fantasy whether David actually lives with us all the time.'

'My dear!' said Vita, realising Catherine meant it. 'You're talking about a raving queen!'

'It's just a fantasy. I like it. It's something, and something is better than nothing. He pretended I was joking. Just as well, I suppose.'

Vita took the coffee off the stove and brought it over.

'Who would have thought, when we were growing up, that it would be like this?' Catherine said. 'Well, it's good to have you. We talked about you.'

'Oh good, what about me?'

'About your job. Everyone's interested in it. I said there must be something wrong with it, but I can't work out what.'

'I can't either.'

'If I ever had any doubts, it's because I was worried at first—about how you'd be treated. By the men.'

'Oh sure! What about how you're treated in a straight office job, always being scrutinised for proof of incompetence, irrationality and willingness to fuck? And how much do you get? Whereas my clients, my dear, are often so courteous and do their best to keep me happy and order my favourite drink.'

'Everyone was wondering how you were coping with attitudes to it. *Their* own attitudes, they meant. Men don't like it.'

'Why would poofters mind? Why would anyone, anyway? I mean, it's what I do, and that's it. Who needs an attitude?'

Vita carried the cups over to the table. Catherine fiddled with cigarettes and sat by the window. 'Do you mind talking about it?' she asked.

'I don't mind with you, you can say anything. Usually it's no fun; I just like proving I've always got an answer. At least *you* don't start off by saying you're thinking of taking it up yourself, like some girls.'

Catherine gave a look of utter disbelief. 'I could no more do what you're doing than...*fly*.'

It was true. And still Catherine always made Vita feel that she respected Vita's choices. As for the whoring, Catherine had said, 'I wouldn't take a point of view if my life depended on it,' which Vita thought was the most sensible remark she'd heard on the subject.

Vita poured the coffee and Catherine twisted another cigarette into the holder that accentuated her look of deliberate and conservative elegance—the French roll, linen suits—a look emphatically unfashionable.

'Not for any money,' said Catherine. 'Have any of those girls decided to go ahead?'

'No, their boyfriends won't let them, or it's not the feminist thing to do. Guess what they ask most, about why you shouldn't?'

'Let me think...'

'They say, "What if you meet someone you *know*?"'

'Oh? Of course. Fascinating. Last thing I'd think of.'

Four common questions:

Q: Why did you decide to take it up?

A: For the money of course, what else?

Q: But you could probably get a really good job.

A: I've *had* really good jobs. I don't like to type or get up early and I have an authority problem. The solution was classical.

Q: What about society's attitudes?

A: I spit on society's attitudes.
Q: It's really anti-feminist, isn't it?
A: But it's winning the war between the sexes.

Oh yes, feminism. But the question really was: who's winning? Sometimes Vita got the approving verdict: 'Make them pay!' Other times she was challenged with the proposition that selling women's bodies is oppressing and degrading. Well, sure it was, she'd agree, if that's the way you see it. For those who *believe* they have no choice, it feels the same as *having* no choice at all. But some of us think that prostitution serves our own interests. If the rules are that it must appear to serve men's interests, so much the better, it's an advantage to our side. Vita could have pointed out that she was working for a business owned and controlled by a woman. Pamela had only the most cynical and pragmatic recognition of the power and authority of men; she had as little regard for girls who 'gave it away' and said she thanked the Lord for making men think they need sex in a way women don't. That was the weapon on her side.

Vita could never explain the motivations of her clients—they were as infinitely variable as they were monotonous. She could not claim to hate them while understanding even part of their desire. You know how horny it can be, she would point out, being alone in a hotel room in a strange city. You start wishing for the perfect stranger—someone who will just walk in the door, make love like an angel and disappear. She'd had that fantasy herself— remote and improbable as it now seemed. These days people are urged to 'live out' their fantasies, to make their dreams come true. Still, when you do, you might agree that more tears are shed over answered prayers.

'There's this other likely scenario that's meant to make me reconsider,' Vita said. 'Finding a one true love: a torrid mutual passion and then my shameful confession leading to the agonising end of the romance.'

'Oh, really.' Catherine looked disbelieving again. 'As if you could have romance with someone who didn't know.'

'Well, quite, but since when has romance been the point? How long since you've had romance?'

'People have "Relationships" instead.' They'd been over all this before. 'At least,' Catherine said, 'you're doing *something*.'

Vita went on thinking she knew all the answers.

Three more common questions:

Q: What if you fell in love with one of your clients?

A: I'm not the type to go falling in love with someone who telephones for call-girls in his spare time.

Q: What if you fell in love with someone who didn't know. Would you tell him?

A: Mr Right always understands.

Q: Aren't you frightened of meeting someone you know?

A: What would I have to be afraid of? He'd be there, too.

PART TWO

15

It's You

Vita would say she didn't go to parties very much and think it was funny that she had gone to that one. Sometimes it would seem like a good idea to go, just because you'd been asked. Even if it was not your close friends, more a matter of Introductions and Conversation Groups and the social chat that gave you only the choice of being polite or rude.

A large house, the whole ground floor open, washed in light from both ends. Day. Early summer. Scattered colour: shrubs in pots inside and out, bowls of flowers, paintings, brightness in the women's clothes to celebrate the brightness of the days.

Vita was sitting on the back terrace, drinking wine and soda, explaining her relationship to their host, an art dealer. An old friend from university had married him. No, she wasn't involved in Art. A man began to tell her to invest in Aboriginal art. Bark paintings, he said. The really good ones would soon be gone, she should invest soon. He had an art gallery, too, and she was to come over some day and he would show them to her. If she were free during the day. What did she do? 'Oh,' she said, 'I'm between careers right now.'

The small crowd in the kitchen was regrouping itself as new arrivals performed overtures beyond. Her eyes passed over three men standing near the door and kept moving to return to the talking head in front of her, but mentally her stare was riveted to the features of the tall, fair man in the middle. A siren wail, silence, a second, the shock over. She might not have missed a word. The destruction of Aboriginal culture...the Americans bought first...they'd be too costly soon...

'Excuse me,' she said, a moment later.

She must have passed close to the men she had noticed, but did not look. He might have seen her on her way to the bathroom.

A lavatory seat was the place for a sudden, urgent need for solitary consideration of the predicament at hand. If it were a predicament. The tall, fair man was Brian Castle and just the other night Violet had been sent on a booking to Brian Castle at his apartment. It was a night she had been thinking about ever since, and here he was now. This was a new situation. This was what she'd been asked, 'what if...'

She stared at the mirror; made some faces. She drank from the tap. She wondered about her nervousness as she subdued it. What was the name of this confusion? Might she suppose this was a self-evident embarrassment...it's what they always asked: what if you met someone you knew? What if Violet walked into a hotel room and found...who? The man next door, her dentist, Daddy? This was the same thing, the other way around; Vita meeting someone Violet knew. So? So, how did one act? There was no authority on etiquette that could tell you. It must be a pretend-we-haven't-met situation, musn't it? Her job was something a gentleman wouldn't refer to, for the lady's sake. They would hardly shriek with delighted recognition and gaily tell their conversation group, 'We've met before; an extraordinary way, listen...'

Good grief! This was a classical Embarrassing Moment for him, too, wasn't it? Would his friends assume that in the course of things one rang for a call-girl sometimes? Still, they probably wouldn't be keen to bump into that same call-girl at a party the next Sunday. He was going to feel in the range put-out to horrified at the sight of her, wasn't he? How would she know? Men's minds worked in ways incomprehensible to the rest of us. Didn't they?

And something else was strange: no man had ever seen both Vita and Violet...and she was about to talk to the man who would score that solitary distinction.

What a thrill to face the music, dance or no dance. Out of the bathroom, to the kitchen. The best part of the party goes on in the kitchen. She strode into his gaze.

'It's you,' he said. He did not appear one bit put out.

A fleeting acknowledgement—recognition—flashes in the eyes, even if the mind is unwilling. Except, perhaps, in the very best

60

actors who have had more time to prepare. Still, she could make it clear that non-recognition was her choice.

'Oh, hello,' she said uncertainly, offering an unconvincing haven't-we-met-but-where look. This conversation group was made up of only two, she was thankful to note.

'How are you?' he asked, warmly, familiarly.

'Fine,' was the best she could do. How did one begin conversations with strangers at parties? No fabulous first lines prepared. 'My name's Vita,' she said brightly.

'Vita,' he repeated. Odd expression—quizzical, she supposed. Violet in the city, Vita in the country. Why did she think of tables turning?

'I'm a friend of Robyn's. I've seen you in a play.' Stupid, yet correct.

'We are pretending we haven't met before,' he stated, cottoning on.

Acknowledged by a long pause; then she smiled her teasing, sideways, Violet smile. 'You see, it wasn't me.'

'I see,' he said, amused. 'The secret identity, like a hidden violet.'

'Not all that secret exactly,' she said. 'Separate. A separate identity.'

'I've thought about you,' he said. 'It was a good night, wasn't it?'

'Brian,' said a male voice behind her, and the conversation group was expanded. Male voices were always interrupting just when you were about to get somewhere.

'So, are you working at the moment?' Vita offered, and he followed that tack and began talking about the television work he'd just done. Someone passing heard a familiar name and joined in too and Vita stepped back into the party and stared at a bark painting while she remembered the night they met.

61

16

Flashback

She had been to the cinema with Catherine to see a double feature. It was late when they got back to Vita's: she had some very good grass. She hadn't intended to work that night, but Pamela rang.

'There's no-one left and it's a very good booking.'

'All right,' she said. Catherine was leaving, dope made her sleepy. It made Vita excited.

'Going out? If there's one reason I couldn't do your job,' Catherine said, 'it's the hours you keep. Do you often go out this late?'

'Later, too. I could never get up as early as you do. . .um, will I put on something else? Maybe the top needs to look a bit more tarty. Roll another one, I'm not going far.' She took out her high heels and splashed scent over herself. She was already wearing gorgeous underclothes: a personal indulgence learned from Violet and taken up full time.

Catherine watched the transformation, entertained, fond. 'To think they get *you*,' she said. 'They ring up for someone they don't know and they get you.'

'Not exactly,' Vita replied. 'They get—someone.' She struck a pose, mascara in hand.

'Still, do they know how lucky they are?'

'Well, guess what happened once. I had a booking and I got there and he asked me in and then after one minute he said, "I'm sorry, I've changed my mind," and showed me the door.'

'I suppose that was like saying "here's the bad news *and* the good news," ' Catherine said.

As they left, Catherine said, 'Have a good time. Or shouldn't I say that? Do you ever have a good time?'

'The best time I have is when I walk out saying, "Oh, that was all right, he was easy." ' Vita the posturing cynic.

'Doesn't show much hope for our relationships with men.'

'Our *what*?' said Vita, in theatrical disbelief.

'I know what you mean. Well, hope it's easy.'

On the way, she looked at the name again: Brian Castle. Did it sound familiar? Strangely familiar. Familiarly strange.

The address was a large, new, waterside block. Only one apartment had all its lights on—that would be it. She pressed the button. No voice over the intercom but the door buzzed and opened. She took the lift.

He was standing at the door.

Had she seen him before? Where? She looked around. There was something odd about the place. It was as if no-one really lived there. There weren't many things lying around—few clues to the everyday life. Music was playing loudly.

'Oh nice, I like this.'

'It's Manhattan Transfer.'

'I know.' It was easy, she was in the mood. 'What are you drinking?'

'I was about to offer you one.' She had been hasty. He indicated a flagon. 'Would you like a glass of wine?'

'I'd prefer water—with a dash of whisky.'

'There's only this wine. I'm sorry, darling. I would have had whatever you wanted but I haven't spent a lot of time here lately.'

'If that's all there is, I'll try to forget my Serious Doubts about flagons. And their age.'

He took out another glass and filled it, then he went to fix up the business.

'It's fifty dollars, but that's only. . .' she began.

He interrupted; he knew what was what. 'Plus whatever you write. It's blank.' He hardly looked, signed quickly, no fuss. Good.

'Where have you been, away?'

The unlived-in flat was because he had been working in the States; a theatre season, then some television. He was an actor, so of course they talked about various shows and films. He asked her what she had seen, her opinions; welcome questions like that.

63

Time passed. They kept on talking. She remembered about hurrying, but there didn't seem any point. It was very late.

He told her about a film actress he had seen on stage. She wasn't any good, he said, you have to be big, project yourself; and he made large gestures and filled the room to a distant back row. And on film it's all here, he said, gesturing closely around his face.

She sat there, wide-eyed, knowing it was a game. His movements reminded her that she had seen him before. He had been in some play she couldn't remember the name of. It must have been two years ago; three maybe. Plays left only the dimmest traces in her memory—she was more likely to remember who went and who had drinks after.

She kicked off her shoes and threw her legs over the arm of the sofa—the same way she sat at home. He seemed entirely relaxed too, and, at a point in the conversation, they smiled at each other, holding each other's gaze. This was more than 'easy'. He had lovely eyes—full of humour, but intense, too. He looked good, a kind of sexy gracefulness. He was nice. She nearly forgot he was paying for her.

She told him about the films she'd seen that night—one of them was a local production and a fashionable success, but she hadn't enjoyed it.

'Depressing little film?' he suggested.

'Really,' she said. 'What a waste to walk out thinking my life is far more interesting. What is this conspiracy of pessimism?'

'Exactly,' he said. It was only what the situation required, but it was *more* than agreement: it looked like a kind of acknowledgement of herself that included Violet as the façade.

'So you saw that tonight?'

'Yes,' she said. 'Then I went home and then I was asked to go out in the middle of the night and visit a man I'd never met before!'

That look again—amused and knowing. It was as if he recognised the humorous, even ludicrous, element in their temporary alliance. It was as if they shared a very secret, inexpressible joke: that this absurd form of entertainment had been devised entirely for their own enjoyment.

This sense of conspiracy was quite new to her.

'What were you doing tonight?' she asked.

He had been to a new play. He thought she should go and see it, too. No, he didn't think it would be very popular, but some people would like it. 'People like us,' he said.

Violet had never met a man who said, 'People like us.'

She understood when people said, 'Like them.'

'Now, tell me about yourself,' he said. 'Is Violet your real name?'

'A name's just something to answer to, I always say.'

She looked at him. She drank some more. He told her he'd met some people he knew at the theatre that night. He talked about some of them. He had stayed back and had a drink or two. Then he had returned to his apartment and opened a flagon of wine. That was when he had telephoned Pamela.

'Why did you call Pamela?' Violet often asked that. She might mean: rather than another? She might mean: why do you use these services?

'A friend gave me the number,' he said cheerfully. She could not imagine the exchange. He seemed completely relaxed. Quite charming, she thought; this charming actor. She didn't want to talk any more.

Violet was often asked about herself and usually bubbled some reply. Now she felt as if Violet were being given cues meant for another character. It made her uneasy—not an unpleasant uneasiness—more a waking and wanting and he looked good and after all what was she here for, type uneasiness. Perhaps it had something to do with indefinable desires that sought an object...

'Well isn't it nice,' she whispered, as they drew closer, 'for such a meeting to turn out to be such a pleasure.'

'Don't flatter me, darling, or I'll...fall asleep on you.' Flattery puts him to sleep? she thought. It sounded funny, the way he said it, and they laughed a little before the first kiss...

She left straight after—it was the only thing to do. No goodbyes.

She kept thinking about him. He was different.

'This man the other night,' she told Catherine, 'was gorgeous. He was so *nice*. He was nice to be with.'

Catherine got straight to what was wrong with him: the fact that he phoned for call-girls. Vita had better realise she was lucky if she *didn't* see him again, Catherine said. No good could ever come of it. To get emotionally involved—that would be the most dangerous thing in the job. As dangerous as getting emotionally deadened. See what a dangerous thing it is? The sooner Vita started doing something else, the better. No, she didn't know what; she, herself, was going back to work at the ABC—what else could she do?—and that was prostitution, if you like.

She then firmly changed the subject.

Then Vita went to a party on a Sunday afternoon and there he was: Brian. They contrived to have a few words together, and she turned away when they were interrupted. She stared at a bark painting and remembered the night, the way she had wanted him to kiss her, the way they had kept on kissing...

Someone was beside her. What had he said? Oh, he'd asked her what she thought of the painting.

'Not what you'd expect,' she said, distractedly, ruder than she meant to be. 'Where's my bag?'

There was Brian across the room with a group of people around him. He looked at her, too. His studied charm made her nervous in a faint, silly way she'd rather not think about. Her life strictly excluded any personal attractions and that was that. Must be time to go. She found her bag and left.

He watched her go.

17

The Girls

Susie had it all worked out.

'He's coming back on the seventeenth and I'm going to say, do you really want me to go on working? And he'll have to say no. And I'll say, well, you have to take care of it, because my expenses...how much do you think I should say?'

Pamela had seen this before. 'If he gets a divorce he won't have that kind of money any more.'

'I'll say,' said Susie, 'I'll say, how can I love you and be working at the same time?'

Faye barely stirred her languid body or her heavy, bronzed eyelids. 'Yeah, hold on to him—there's too many who'd rather be living off you.'

Pamela was attending to the phones. 'Hello, yes...I'm sorry, I can't help you.' She hung up. An unacceptable address, an unacceptable request.

'Want a mandie?' Faye whispered to Violet. She offered generously. Violet hesitated and Amber came into the office. 'I'm just in time, the car just pulled up outside.'

Amber was a tousled-haired earth-mother type, older than the others, with less glamour but more enthusiasm than any of them. She was very popular and didn't even wear high heels.

Pamela looked at her watch. 'You're late, Amber, that's not like you.'

The car, with the four of them inside, slowly edged its way through the Cross, past its crowds of tourists, touters, bikies and the odd local pushing through with a shopping bag. Susie stared at the streetwalkers: big-breasted flaunters strutting their stuff, transsexuals posing in doorways, and drug addicts curled up inside their scanty rags, heavy-eyed, nodding.

'How could they?' Susie said, all prim outrage. 'Standing out on the street like that for anyone to see.'

Not like us princesses, us chauffeur-driven dolls who keep off the streets and can even say no, within reason.

'They're just prostitutes,' Faye muttered.

'So are we,' said Violet.

Susie and Faye were shocked. The driver's face twitched. Faye took out her make-up and peered into a tiny mirror.

'They did this study,' Amber said, all seriousness, 'in three American cities, looking at five levels of prostitution, and they found the girls on the street would say that money was the only possible reward and they would see it as a matter of survival, not so much choice. Then when you go...'

'Might start off as a choice,' mumbled Faye.

'Where did you read this?' Violet asked, with real interest.

'What kind of blusher is that? Is it waterproof?' Susie asked.

It was the year advertising executives would have two girls each. The champagne was French, but they let Faye order some milk instead, and some gooey cake, which was all she'd eat. The man who had won first choice asked Susie, who took Faye with her. 'I always do doubles with Faye,' she said. The other man showed Violet and Amber to his room and went off to fetch something. What? They didn't care.

Violet and Amber looked around and passed each other the lubricant in the bathroom. 'Faye believes all those victim pictures,' said Amber. 'She thinks she's in a trap. I've tried to talk to her.'

'Talk to me,' Violet said. 'Remind me why we're doing this.'

Doing this: smearing our pussies with cold jelly, so he'll really think we're hot for him; this dopey routine. Look at Faye: her fantasy is the glamour of a self-destruction she believes is inevitable, and maybe she's right.

'Why did you start?' asked Amber.

'Best job offer I had at the time,' said Violet. 'It's *work*, but everyone has to make a judgement. Why can't it just be a job, like everyone else's?'

Amber looked hard at her. 'You can get a lot out of this. Self-esteem. Like that friend of yours—I'm sorry about that, by the way.'

'Oh, Liz was amazing. I started through her.'

'Liz was Jill?'

'Yeah. Tell me about this therapy deal you're doing.'

'Surrogate therapy. I take a few clients for a psychiatrist. I'm going to do the proper training in California next year.'

'What do *your* friends think?'

'Is that what's bugging you?' Amber looked at her again. 'Are they real friends?'

The man came back into the room, looking very pleased with himself.

'Won't be long!' Amber called from the bathroom, shutting the door on him, leaving him fiddling with his box of fancy attachments. 'What do these friends say?'

'I'll be sorry, no-one will love me, I make them look bad.' Violet shrugged. 'The usual, no?'

'Lady, come and talk to me later. I have a beautiful boyfriend who really knows how special he is because of what I do.' She flung open the bathroom door.

Susie and Faye were already in the elevator that stopped at their floor. 'I told you they all take the same time,' said Susie.

'This is about immediate gratification,' Amber kept explaining, 'and, as a therapist, I work on delayed gratification, completely different...'

A young woman in high heels and a very frilly dress was waiting for the elevator and hastily attempting to switch off her shrill little beeper as they all got out in the lobby.

Violet saw the TV magazine at the newsstand, and stared at it. The other girls were exchanging final notes. The other man had had a box of 'aids', too.

'It does show it's *us* they have to please...' Amber said.

There was a picture of Brian Castle on the cover, as inside there was a story about the television series. This hotel newsstand was closed. She decided to stop at the all-night newsstand on the way home.

'...*we're* in control,' Amber was saying, '*we* get paid, *we* get the flattery, *we* walk out with it all.'

18
Other Roles

'Violet? Can you go out? A repeat for you.'

'Who?'

'Brian Castle.'

Pause.

'He made sure you were available.'

Pause.

'What's the matter?'

Violet had reported he was 'good' after his first booking. Too late to pretend anything else. She could suggest sending someone else, but why?

'Nothing. Where is it?'

'Got a pen?'

The address was the same.

'Half an hour,' she repeated mechanically, and hung up.

He had rung and asked to see Violet again. How about that. How curious. Confusion called for some pacing around but she had to get dressed. She was about to play a new game: the one she hadn't bargained for; the one she shouldn't play.

Abruptly, she stopped searching for her high heels. All she had to do was ring Pamela back, admit her previous hesitation and tell her the truth: that she had met him somewhere else. That was reason enough to refuse a booking. It wasn't too late. She couldn't possibly go.

She would be late. Why shouldn't she go? This was a new game, after all. It could be fun. Life was not dull! She took out the reddest lipstick. The situation was slightly bizarre—how could you miss out on that? The thought of him waiting for her now produced a ridiculous sensation: elation, anticipation, exhilaration! It certainly could be a whole lot worse. She decided against the Chanel and sprayed herself with Joy.

71

It was as before—the buzzer, the lift, Brian waiting at the door. He said it was lovely to see her. 'Don't you look beautiful,' he said. He was doing all right so far.

She walked in. 'I'm not sure I should be here. This isn't in the rules, you know.'

'Don't be silly, darling. Would you like a drink? There's Scotch this time.' Full points. Self-possessed, Scotch this time. They were both doing all right so far.

'Pamela told me you asked for me. Why did you?'

'I thought it would be nice to see you.'

'Me? You did ask for Violet.'

'I am not confusing the player with the part,' he said, handing her the drink. 'And I'd like,' he added, 'to see you play seven other roles.'

'All in time,' she said. 'You asked for Violet this time.' She sat down. 'Before I forget. . .' She took out her credit card forms. 'This part is in the rules.' She wrote the full amount; he had his card ready and signed quickly.

Well, she was there. She had chosen to go. Too late to change that. Figure it out tomorrow. Tomorrow at Tara, Violet.

'Cheers.' He is all calm affability. She is relaxed. 'Let's have some music.' He is all courteous anticipation. She smiles. 'Something especially for you.' He is charm itself. She surrenders. Violet surrenders to the moment. Not a bad moment. Good Scotch; good music.

'Wonderful,' Violet said, laughing, holding out her glass for more. 'What were you doing this evening before I came?'

'What were *you* doing? Let me guess. . . You were lying on your violet-coloured, violet-scented silk sheets, eating chocolates and painting your toenails.'

'Pink. I'd been trying all day to get just the right colour; I had to keep changing it. This one's right, isn't it? Not too pink. Lovely with the gold.' She posed, one foot extended. She wore high heeled gold sandals, a gold ankle chain, blue silk pyjamas. Flashy. She could be so *piquante*, so vivid.

He is both Violet's audience and leading man; both the judge of her performance and the conjuror who conspires in the illusion and makes it all seem as real as anything that makes you smile or cry or your heart beat faster. . .

He held out his hand, they danced, moving easily together. They were together performing and watching a staged romance. She was no longer the voyeur, observing and calculating; here, she was his accomplice in that shared joke: an absurd masquerade invented to be their own secret pleasure.

'You have a dangerous effect on me,' he said, pressing her closer. They kept on kissing, breathing through their kisses. This was something to put aside all thoughts for.

'I love what you do to me,' she whispered, teasingly sincere.

'You make it happen,' he said.

She touched him there and there and moved her head to hide her face when he held her again. As if she wouldn't kiss him. As if there were any point in remembering any of those rules and strategies. As if anything mattered outside of this moment.

She took her clothes into the bathroom. She came out dressed, and went to the telephone.

'You're not going,' he said, as she stood at the bedroom door.

'I am.'

'Why don't you stay? Stay the night. I'd love to make love to you in the morning.' She'd love to stay. She'd better go. She would be someone else in the morning.

'No,' she said, too emphatically, 'no,' more ambiguously, 'I can't.'

'Leave your phone number, I'll take you out to dinner. As friends.'

'I don't know you well enough.'

'Darling, haven't you heard of instant attraction?'

'Instant attraction is one thing, knowing you better is another,' she said, not at all sure it was true.

'Knowing you better is the idea,' he said. 'Come here.' She sat on the edge of the bed. 'I'd like to see you again. It doesn't have to be this way.'

'I don't know...' Was this just her stubbornness, a habit of disbelief? She never gave her private number to clients. But then, they were never like this. Just how different could this one be? And would he then also be available to her?

'Is there someone...a boyfriend?'

'No! I live alone and that's the way I like it.' Where was the piquancy?

'I don't want to take anything away from you,' he said. 'Miss Independent. It could be very nice. Look, I know this isn't the way it usually happens.'

'What happens?'

'I thought a bit of love and affection never hurt anyone... You can have as many commercial affairs as you like, but when it comes to emotions...'

'I don't know...' She felt she was losing. If she resisted, she was denying herself. If she agreed, she was giving in.

'Just let me call you; if you don't want to go out I can ring and say hello from time to time.'

'Hello is what I say when I pick up the phone. Goodbye.' She leant over and gave him a kiss on each cheek. Then, believing she was still not deciding anything, she recited her number and walked out the door, leaving him, and leaving for herself only an insistent question.

19
A Man's Voice

One day she stares at her ringing phone sitting importantly among coloured pens and teacups, and she knows.

'Is that Vita or Violet?'

'Which do you want?'

'I can always pick up clues, darling. How's the night-life?'

'Some would say it's great. You know, a pleasure. . . I love the sound of your voice.'

'I love the sound of your voice. What have you been doing?'

'The usual—sitting by the phone, you know. Wondering which one to be, I suppose. What about you? Seen any films?' Bright and chatty, keep it going.

'*All* the films,' and he reels off the name of every show in town, adding 'nice little film' once or twice. He can do it, too, make easy phone conversation. They are great support acts for each other.

'Well, it's good you've got work, I suppose,' she says. 'Sounds like a lot. Do you like it?'

'I love it, I love working. Next to sex,' he says, 'I love work more than anything.'

'Why don't you be like me, then you can love them both the same?'

He is amused. 'I think there's a greater demand for ladies, darling. . . What have you got on?'

'An ad for Joy. Lots of Joy. I'm lying on my bed,' she adds, brightly.

'Darling, I wish I was in it.'

'What a nice thought.'

'Are your legs wide open?' Does he really say that?

'No, they're *tightly* crossed.' Ambiguous, she hopes.

'Uncross them! My cock's getting hard just talking to you,' he whispers. 'Wouldn't you love to put it in your mouth?'

'Don't do this to me,' she says. 'Yes, I would, in my mouth, then I'd lick your...' and she leans back on the cushions, cradling the phone between head and shoulder, her hands moving on her breasts. 'Stop it!' she says insincerely. 'Oh God, I can feel it...it is, I am, I am,' she whispers to him, heated, sincere, 'so wet, listen,' and she thinks, brilliant! crazy! impossible! 'I don't know if I'm going to laugh or come,' she giggles. 'Is this dirty talk?' And she listens some more, moaning a little, moaning, 'God, yes, don't, I can't stand it.' And then she grasps the phone in one hand and says firmly, 'Seriously, I've got to go. I'm on duty, you know.'

'You must have a night off some time.'

'I do if I arrange it before.'

'Let's arrange it then... When can I see you?'

'I'll let you know. Who do you want?' she giggles. 'Vita or Violet?'

'It's you, darling, it's all you.'

She giggles and hangs up. She goes to the mirror and sees a kaleidoscope of expression. 'No,' she says, 'I can't choose one.'

20
'Hello?'

There go the pips; it's long distance.

'I hope you're wearing lots of Joy.'

'It's you.'

'Of course it's me. In the middle of the desert thinking of you.'

'Where are you?'

He is in a motel in a country town, working on the film he had told her about.

'You've always given local content new meaning,' she says.

'No talent can be totally hidden.'

She skips a beat, awkwardly. 'So, this film, what is it, more period costume drama? Have you got a nice part?' Now they could have a long partyish conversation about his career, his agent, his best profile, his big break, his fame.

'Very nice part. You're nice, too. . .'

She does not interrupt.

'Do you miss me?' he continues.

'I was starting to think I'd never see you again.' And wondering if it could be so bad.

'Don't be negative, darling.' Glib, she thinks. The practised assurance of a practised playboy. 'How is everything? Are you having a holiday?'

'I'm still here. Waiting, as usual.' The sound of distance. 'Brian,' it's the first time she's used his name, 'I'm glad you rang.'

'What have you been thinking?'

'Thoughts, of course. . . After the state you left me in last time, should I think of you?'

'Just as well you're not here, I'd never get to work.'

Oh really? she thinks, the work and women conflict? 'We ladies are a distraction,' she says drily. 'Well, I'd like to come over and distract you. When's the next plane?'

'Darling...' She's thought about the way they talk to each other: endearments that are façades for what they mean, and they know they are façades. But aren't these façades also replicas of the truth protected behind them? Darling, darling.

Someone knocks on his door. 'I'll have to go now, darling, to look at rushes. I'll call you again soon...'

'Yes, when you get back.' She could say 'tomorrow'.

'And I'll see you then.'

'Yes,' doubtfully, wanting more assurance. 'But you know, I have these commitments...' What commitments?

'Of course.' Of course. What does he think she means?

They kiss the air, and hang up. Now what is she to believe? What can either of them believe, knowing she had so often protested her pleasure with her fingers crossed and one eye on the clock, lying.

I think of you, I love your voice. True.

They had met out of a shared faith in daring. True or false?

She looks at the *TV Guide*.

He makes her think he wants her for her unique quality. Me me me. The Real Me is Wanted. True or false?

She'll watch television tonight.

He isn't bad, either. Smart enough to have her wondering about him now.

He's dangerous to know. He's a skilful manipulator. He wants to control the situation. True or false?

Why stop now, she tells herself. Play it out to the end. Any end. If there is an end.

21
Timing

The *TV Guide* had what he would call a 'nice little story'. His career. He would apear on Wednesday. Also has been seen in. Soon to be seen in. Nice little part. An actor to watch.

She was having a kind of farewell evening with Catherine, who had her plane ticket and traveller's cheques—she was spending a month away before beginning a new job and a new life.

'Would you like to come over here?' Catherine had said. 'I couldn't bear a restaurant or social intercourse. I'll cook, we'll watch TV...' One of their favourite kinds of evenings.

They sat bathed in television light. Catherine used to work with the series' director, so she filled Vita in on the gossip.

'Do you know any of these people, too?' Vita asked, waving at the actors on the screen.

'No, do you?'

'No, oh, I've met him,' she said casually, as Brian appeared.

'He'd be gay, wouldn't he,' said Catherine, meaning he was attractive.

'Huh,' said Vita, meaning anything. He was, yes, different, all the subtle adjustments to suggest another character, but there was his voice, the odd gesture, the way he moved his eyes; something that was Brian; some essentiality showing through any disguise.

In the other room the phone rang. Catherine went to answer it and Vita heard him ask for her and then saw herself glide into the night to meet him and then...

Of course the phone could not have been for her and it wasn't, but she took a look at the fantasy she had spiralled into and felt as if she were host to a desire over which she felt no control or understanding. Hostess, surely. Hostess to desire.

The girls decided to play music instead. Catherine sat on the sofa, twisting a cigarette into her holder, Vita sat on the floor.

The spinach quiche had tasted delicious; the tray was piled with banana cake and herbal tea. They rolled a mixture of grass and hash. They promised they would write.

'I'll miss you,' said Vita, meaning their rituals, their favourite place for coffee, their part of the beach, their chats about what really mattered.

'Why don't you come too?' said Catherine. 'You must be able to afford it by now.'

'I just might,' said Vita. 'But I'll go for longer, once I stop feeling there's unfinished business around. I hate unfinished business more than anything.'

'Can't you finish it in Europe? You keep saying you want to go. There's nothing here for either of us. I mean Australian men...well, don't let's start on that.'

'Let's not, please. Do you think they're better in Europe? Better dressed at least. I have wanted to go for ages actually but I don't know about the timing. I must get my transits done. Timing is everything, isn't it? But then, when you're too late for one thing, you're just in time for something else, I suppose.'

'The biorhythms were a dud, weren't they? Vita, your job...' ventured Catherine, never quite sure around this topic. 'How long do you think you can go on doing it?'

The Burn-Out Question. Hookers were supposed to be susceptible to rapid burn-out; it had a high rating as an occupational hazard of the 'helping' professions and led to suicidal psychiatrists, alcoholic priests and drug-addicted social workers. The Those who Gave Too Much group, who thought their clients were the proof of human nature.

'I can do it for a while, what's it matter? How else can I have a high standard of living and still say,' a classic obscene gesture, *
'that.'

'What do you want?'

'I want to be happy,' answered Vita, without hesitation.

'That's silly, happiness isn't a goal.'

'What is it then?'

'It's a result...'

'Well I want whatever results in being happy all the time. Anyway, it should be a result, because I believe in happy endings. Lots of songs and costumes and a happy ending.'

'Yes,' said Catherine, but it was more a question. 'But what is an ending? I thought it was a happy ending when I got married, and then there I was, three years later, burning his favourite painting and tearing up every photograph of him.'

'That wasn't the ending either. One story stopped at the wedding. That's one happy ending. Or it stops at any point where you decide it was worth it. You know, call it a learning experience.'

Later, they turned the television on again, for the late movie—*Fedora*.

'What's this supposed to mean?' said Vita, during the second last commercial break.

'If you put on a disguise you get stuck with it,' said Catherine, pouring more wine. 'This idea,' she said with sardonic delight, 'that people want to be loved for who they really are. I reckon Mr Right's the one who loves me for who I'd like to be.'

'My favourite question,' said Vita, 'is: Do you prefer love or irony?'

22

Violet's Life Goes On, Too

Violet's life goes on, too, with those charades called sex, those other charades called companionship. Blind dates each night. It's immaterial whether they are more alike than different; each skin has its own texture and it's always the texture of skin. Her lipstick leaves its tattoo trails over chests and shoulders (busily pressing her lips there and there to avoid the most intimate embrace). She pays tribute to the performance of desire and satisfaction, her detached self-noting; amidst her groans she checks her watch behind his shuddering back, or her self in the mirror looking over in understanding; she darts her eyes over the details of disarray in the hotel room: a cool search for clues, messages.

'I really think you enjoyed that,' she is told, proudly.

'Why wouldn't I enjoy it,' she whispers flatteringly, 'when it's someone as cute as you?' or, as kind, or, well, he always has some quality obviously begging acknowledgement.

She knows the odours of bodies—those in good health and of good integrity, and those surrendered to habits of violation and punishment. She recognises the smell of decay; another rotting corpse, she thinks.

This is too dreadful, she muses occasionally. How could I do this? I really ought to stop. But it's never for long; soon she's gone and it's all forgotten. And she has earned more in a night than she used to earn in a whole week, which is compensation—is, in fact, the whole point.

But the smell of life is something else, something she can acknowledge and enjoy freely, too—why not, when there are men who provide an enactment of a possible world in which brief romances are held between travelling strangers who can love each other well in a chosen interlude. She liked to meet the masculine whores, the dealers, the oil and mining men, the mercenaries. There was an odd respect between them—she, the feminine mercenary, they, restless, taut, tanned men, who liked to work hard, get high with companionable sex-mad women, and move on quickly to get high in some other part of the world. They belonged to an international country, and so, romantically, they had those eyes that were used to looking at far horizons. These careless, extravagant evenings let them believe that they could escape the sadness shared by the rest of the world, the sadness of love without love, of a parting most inevitable at the moment of coming together.

Violet's private life remained elusive, she watched those who wondered construct their own version. One of these went: 'I'm sorry you're doing this, love. I bet you've had a hard life.' The implications of their sorriness didn't bear consideration.

'You're a smart lady,' was another version, easier to take. 'This is what I'd be doing if I was a female. You should make a lot of money, invest it, and get out and buy a little business of your own.'

The hard-headed business-motive types were easy to deal with. They solicited no shows of affection, employed no endearments and thankfully did not seem to be left wondering what all the fuss was about.

One of them, Steve, was handsome, exacting in bed, but without sentimentality.

'You're an excellent screw, Violet,' he said, too frankly and dispassionately to sound crude, before she left. 'I don't think you'd have any complaints. That's for you,' giving her a tip, 'not for the boss.'

She saw him again. 'They told me you were on again tonight,' he said, when she arrived. 'I don't like to get involved with a lady but I remember that you are an excellent screw and you won't be staying long.' (Long enough for a demanding workout but not long enough to get involved.) 'That's the way,' he approved, when she reminded him of a little matter to get out of the way first. 'Get as much as you can off a bloke beforehand.

The pre-coital gratitude of a man is immense,' he said, counting out notes. 'Get him very horny and he'll pay up immediately. Here's a little something for the taxi-driver and one for you. That one's not for the boss. A man is very grateful when he's all worked up and waiting for it, but he doesn't feel post-coital gratitude.'

'The likes of you make a girl's job easy,' she said lightly.

Sometimes she'd have a run of men who confirmed a belief that men were invented to make a girl's job easy. And she'd go on wondering whether men's thoughts could ever be known, and whether there was a man waiting to answer a question she'd never asked.

She is lying in bed, part of her there playing the relaxed contentment 'afterwards'. The boyfriend question comes up and Violet says no, no boyfriend.

'Well I couldn't have, really,' she says, 'could I, going out every night to meet strange men. It's not a way of life that could include a boyfriend.'

The American says, 'Don't think no man can understand. It is possible. A man *can* love a working girl.'

'Have you?'

'Yes.'

'Tell me. Where did you meet her?'

'In a hotel room in Paris. Like this. Through an agency like yours. I stayed in Paris for two years and lived with her and she went on working. Then she went to New York with me and eventually we split up. She drove me mad after a while.' He offers her a cigarette.

'There's a funny sort of sequel,' he continues. 'I was in Paris again last year and I met another girl. Like this. She kept saying she thought I looked familiar. She asked my name and I told her and she said, "Of course!" It turned out she was a good friend of my former girlfriend and she'd seen photographs of me and heard a lot about me. . . She said, "Let me call her; don't you want to see her?" I said no. For me it was over.'

Violet hears a lot about affairs that are over, marriages that are finished. 'Work was too important to me,' he said one night. 'A man can't love his work and a woman. Only one thing can come first. And in my kind of work,' he said, 'you've got to be ambitious.'

He wasn't the only one. 'I spent all my time working,' another said. 'She got sick of it and left. She always wanted to talk about us, the relationship. I couldn't think in those terms. Women think differently from men.' She made him go on. 'Women always think about what everything means, things you say. They're always thinking about it. Men don't think like that. They have a lot of work to do.'

23

The Americans

'Hi, Pamela, it's Violet. The gentlemen have extended their time.'
Violet was sitting on the edge of the bed, pouting a kiss at her
paying escort.

'How long will you be?'

'They're taking us to dinner and to dance etcetera. We said
about four hours.'

'All right. Ring by twelve, will you, there just might be
something for you later. Everything all right there?' (Have they
paid?)

'They are darling, very nice,' Violet said loudly. (They had.)
'Bye.' She hung up. 'She asked me about you and I said you were
darling,' she announced cheerfully. 'Have you chosen a place?'
The other pair were consulting a list of restaurants. 'Shall I ring,
or do you want to?'

'Let me call room service first, they must have better booze
than in this icebox here.'

'Don't you love the way they talk?' gushed Marilyn. 'I love
going out with Americans, don't you, Violet?'

'We've heard you Australian ladies don't think much of your
men,' proffered Violet's partner for the evening. 'Why is that?'

'Have you heard the expression "Male Chauvinist Pig"?' asked
Marilyn, earnestly. 'That's Australian men. They wouldn't open
your car door, they wouldn't light your cigarette—they're male
chauvinist pigs.'

The Southern gentlemen deplored this state of affairs and pointed
out that back home they were taught to respect and protect their ladies.
Drinks arrived and lots of congratulating and complimenting went
on and finally they ordered a car to take them to the chosen place to
dine and dance. Violet was complimented on her dancing, then,
'Excuse me,' he said, a moment later, 'may I lead?'

'Hi, it's me again—Violet. I'm here with Mr Firestone in his room, and we just got back. He would like to extend for another hour.'

'Tell her I'm not letting you go!' said Mr Firestone.

'Oh well,' said Pamela, 'all right. Although you might have been better off finishing there early, as I've had a request for you.'

'Who?'

'You remember a Brian Castle? He's asked for you before. Never mind, I'll see if he'll see someone else.'

'Oh look, I'll call you again in an hour,' Violet said, suddenly furious at the man with her now. Could she say see if he'll wait in front of him? 'See if he'll wait,' she said.

'You plan on hurrying away?' Mr Firestone asked.

'Of course not,' she said, calculating how soon she could get out of there. 'We've got all the time in the world.'

24

Vita Talks about Funny Things

We were saying only the other night about how you sometimes feel horny all the time and you think you could easily devote your whole life to sex. And then, with just about every opportunity what you actually think is: is this worth it? Is this it? Sex is a funny thing.

But then there are other times—those times when it really is as good as your dreams. Transcendent. Only, then, you're not left feeling satisfied but more aroused. It's as if the more fulfilment and pleasure you get from fucking, the more intense the longing that remains. I don't know.

I've been thinking about Brian Castle. He once asked me what I thought sexual compatibility was. (We had it.) 'A mystery,' I said, having given it a great deal of thought. I've thought some more about it recently. Maybe it's something like having the same kind of fantasy.

Brian. There was a time I got into quite a state about him. It was as if I suddenly didn't have all the answers any more. I would think about him, and go about with that feeling of waiting for something; listening for that special ring to the phone. Anticipation brings strong women undone. 'Piss off,' I'd say, 'who needs it.' But then I'd see his eyes, the way he moved and I'd think some more.

It was the situation that made it so interesting—the way we met. I'd assumed I'd never be able to have any real interest in any of my clients, but there was something about him. What? I don't know. How do you explain these things?

It must have been love. I loved the way we met. I loved the idea that in the enactment of love's oldest parody I found myself caught in some unlikely fascination, some bewitching notion that this was different. I loved the idea of meeting at the level of fantasy.

After I saw him at that party, the intrigue began. Why had he then wanted to see me as 'Violet'? For him I could not conform to the usual requisite fantasy that I was only a good-time-girl, who was mad about money and men and had no existence outside of flutterings in and out of hotel rooms and the occasional apartment at a good address.

He was watching me assume a role.

It led nowhere trying to understand my own feelings. Your emotions go to war with your understanding and your heart is caught in the crossfire; it's like the songs. It was a big moment for me when I realised that all those exciting, longing feelings were actually my own; that my pounding blood, dreaming and distraction were things *I* was doing, and not Violet play-acting. Oh yes, I was all aflame with desire and I hadn't known it was my own.

It was Violet he'd met and asked to see again. And I'd think that his interest, his charm, those sexy promises were meant only for her—only for Violet.

I knew *something* I was doing might not have been a good idea, but I wasn't sure what. I took a look at all the stories about such unconventional liaisons—they all proved that a man who believed the promises of a whore was a fool and was inevitably had; that an unvirtuous woman who believed she could be both purchased and loved was a sad victim and was inevitably broken. I knew these stories had nothing to do with me. I had already decided to start making up some new stories. Maybe a story where Brian knew something I didn't know. Something about me, the intersection that was unknown territory to me.

I knew that my fascination with Brian was really a fascination with myself, my compartmentalised life; and that it was the same for him. We were reflections of each other. . .the thought goes on endlessly.

As endlessly as once I had imagined our next time together, promising myself there'd be no holding back. I must have been relieved and thrilled (could that be it?) to discover I actually had the capability to be truly aroused, to make love with my heart in

89

it, to come over and over, to be a reflection of a delicious combination of skill and passion.

One of my new stories was about living life without being obsessed by The Relationship. Relationships sounded like proposals to get in each other's way. All I could see around me was men and women not getting on. And still everyone was always supposed to be making it with someone.

What most people settled for was not what I had in mind for myself. I kept finding reasons to say so. I wanted a way of life that I had not yet seen. Working for Pamela fitted in with that. And I realise I never saw it as a sexual choice, only an economic one—with the advantage of being an effective 'Up you' gesture to both Mr Right fantasies, even of the liberated kind, and separatist puritans. It also had the advantages of being a job where you Dressed Up, Drank, and Had Fun. Well, it was supposed to be fun.

Compared to what I saw as the options, it had everything going for it: the challenges, the money.

But as for sex, sometimes it would be all right, usually it was nothing. 'Performance' is how the typical man refers to sex. 'Don't know if I can perform. How did I perform? I usually perform better.' And performance is what he gets. All the whores I used to meet would say you had to be an actress. The acting was more fun than the sex.

Then there was Brian.

Maybe I just wanted a different kind of pretending, to see what it was like if, for once, just suppose, I really felt involved, really cared.

Brian was gorgeous. And the fact was, that fucking with him was really something. I never used to be able to explain these things. I still can't. Women I know talk about their lovers and get a look in their eyes, all smug and mysterious and hint at the amazing personal chemistry they have—but only when they're alone together. That's why no-one ever knows what women see in men.

25

Overboard

She called Pamela again from the hotel lobby, jiggling around impatiently.

'Hold on a minute,' Pamela said curtly, and finished on her other phone before returning. 'I've just had Mr Firestone on the other line,' she said. 'He called the minute you left him. He's very displeased. You must have really hurried him.'

Vita answered carelessly. 'He was so quick, I couldn't help it and you told me there's this other job. . .'

'You do *not* let a client see you're hurrying him. I don't know what's come over you.'

'I'm sorry. . .what about B. . .Brian Castle?'

'Well you've got that one, he didn't want to see anyone else. If he's that keen to see you, you should be getting more out of him. Got a pen?'

'I remember it, I'll go now.'

'Ring me when you get th. . .' but before Pamela could finish, Vita had hung up and was jumping into a taxi, ignoring in her haste the people who were already waiting in the queue.

The glass doors, the buzzer reached out familiarly; she pressed hard and long and the automatic doors glided open; she ran across the shiny, empty hallway and kicked the wall as she waited for the lift.

He was at the door and she hurried over. They kissed, long minutes at the door and long minutes step by step across the room, never letting go, pressing closer. He steered her to the bed without releasing the embrace and they kept on kissing. She sighed, she sobbed. She kept all her promises. She held nothing back. She was wholehearted, she was moved. She surrendered, she soared.

'I need a drink of water,' she said. He fetched her one. She sat up in bed and pulled the sheet around her. 'Thank you, you are divine. I'm mad about your body. I feel like jelly now.' She drank the whole glass.

'I'm even more ravishing in my dressing gown,' he said, putting it on and sitting beside her.

She shook her head admiringly. 'To think!' she said, gazing at him with affected amazement. 'All this and heterosexual, too.'

'Thank you,' he said. 'I called you all day. You've got an honest job. Where were you all day?'

How peculiar, she wasn't at home, so he called Pamela. Was it all the same to him? 'I was out for lunch, and all afternoon. I was only home for a minute. Why did you have to pick today?'

'I'm leaving tomorrow.'

'I see, it's not all fun.'

'It's only a few days, and I will be coming back. If you can cope with absences...' She looked away. The moment passed. 'Now,' he said, taking her glass, 'wouldn't you like a proper drink?'

'I don't know. You know what, I'd love some tea. Is that possible?' Of course it was. He found another dressing gown for her and went out to the kitchen.

As she walked into the living room, he picked something up off the table and handed it to her. 'Don't forget this,' he said. His American Express card.

'Oh yes,' she said distractedly, not looking at him, staring at it. She took the form from her bag and began to write on it.

'My pen doesn't work, have you got one?' She felt very odd, as if she'd suddenly been awakened in a strange room.

'Try this.' He brought her a pen. This credit card routine hadn't figured in her fantasies about Brian. So what?

'Thanks,' she said. He went back to the kitchen. She could do one of those scenes where the hooker with the heart of gold hands back the money, the violins play, the girl pleads urgently, 'Please, take it, I couldn't keep it, not this time...' The thought almost made her smile. Anyway, there was Pamela...

She heard the hissing of the kettle, then the steaming water being poured into the pot. How different would all this be if she hadn't run into Brian at that party, if he hadn't known who she really was? All he knew was that she used another name.

He came back from the kitchen with a tray. Again, that graceful, confident way of moving.

'You're an angel,' she said. 'To think you make tea, too.'

'I do have my domestic side.'

'Please, no confessions.'

'It's a very small side.' He sat next to her and signed the form she'd left on the table.

'As for that,' she said, and pointed to the card and the form. She didn't go on. He waited. 'I don't know,' she said. 'I was about to say something; but who wants to be sentimental?'

'Sentimental is my middle name, darling,' he said. Such nonsense, such a pretence of nonsense.

'What I really want to know,' she said, 'is why you make me feel like you do?'

'Sexual compatibility?' He'd be saying relationship next. She frowned. 'It's rare, don't you think?' he asked seriously.

'Very rare,' she answered firmly.

'What do you think it is?'

'A mystery. A complete mystery. Can I pour my tea? I like it weak.'

She paid the most elaborate attention to pouring the tea. He watched her, in that way he had of watching her.

'I'm going to Europe soon,' she said, very, very brightly.

'Sounds like fun. Are you going to all of it?'

'I thought just the famous bits: Paris, Rome, you know.'

'I hope you're being taken in the style you deserve.'

'I'm going alone,' she said indignantly. 'This is *my* trip.'

'A holiday?'

'See what happens.'

'Let me know when you get back.'

She looked at him. They could go on like this forever, promise and only promise. We're sitting here cosily in dressing gowns, she thought absurdly, having tea, so now I can say anything!

'You know, seeing you at that party. . .' she stopped. He waited.

93

'It's made everything different; because it was my private life. Oh, this is so hard to explain.'

'You don't have to explain.'

'Well, it's like... Oh.' She threw back her head, mock-dramatic. 'It was better *before*. I could pretend none of this was happening to me.'

'What a fascinating idea. Who was it happening to?'

'It's like, did anyone ever think you're something you're not and they only see what they think you are?'

'A lot. It's what I get paid for.'

'Oh yes. Me too.' They looked at each other.

Suddenly the phone rang, shrill and violent. They froze for a split second then Brian picked it up.

'Hello?' He held the receiver out. 'It's for you.' She stared at him. 'The boss, I think.' She rolled her eyes, realising what that meant, and took the receiver.

'Hello?'

Pamela's voice was very cold. 'I told you to ring me when you got there.'

'I...I'm sorry, I forgot.'

'What's going on there, Violet? I've lost one very good client because you were too eager to rush to the next. I haven't noticed that this one pays you any more than anyone else. Come over and see me tonight. When are you leaving there?'

Vita looked at Brian then at her feet as she talked into the phone. 'I don't know. I'll have to talk to you tomorrow.'

Pamela had had a hard day. She was furious—in her icy way. 'I want to know what's going on and you'd better get over here to me tonight or you're *out*. You won't get anything this good again, dear. What happened to your attitude?'

'My attitude is, I've *had* this shit and *out* is where I want to be.'

'You owe me money, Violet.'

'You'll get it!' She slammed the receiver down.

Brian was looking both fascinated and uneasy as Vita turned to him, still trying to control her anger.

'I've quit, the game's over.'

94

'Maybe that's a good idea,' he answered, swiftly and smoothly—a superficial, habitual style of response. She felt a sudden, intense fury, took hold of a cup and threw it at him as she screamed, 'How *dare* you! Hypocrite!' then burst into tears, immediately making an immense effort to control herself. He put his arms around her awkwardly and tried to do his bit.

'It's all right, baby, you're all right, don't cry now,' he said. So she recovered with an effort and managed a self-mocking half-smile and a few pats to her face, as if to minimise what she felt.

'Oh, isn't life dramatic... Well, weren't we saying something?'

He busied himself tightening his dressing gown around him. 'Look,' he said, 'maybe you shouldn't be so ready to give it up. Do you want to drive a Volkswagen or a Lamborghini?'

She looked at him uneasily. 'The point is, what I *don't* want— and that's a lot of the games I've played up till now. Including with you.'

'Vita'—he used her name! —'you do what you want for your own reason, but don't do it for me!'

'For you?' She shook her head. 'Why would it be for you?'

'I can't give you any guarantees.'

As she was silent, he probably thought she was hurt or let down, and turned on the charm. 'Darling, you would not find it easy to fit into my way of life. As things are now...' He stopped; he meant that as far as he was concerned, things were okay as they stood.

Okay for him.

'I'm not interested in fitting in with your way of life,' she replied. 'I'm making up my own way of life. My own.' And there was a sense of finality. That was that. It's all very well to think about telling the truth at last, but you have to know what it is. The truth was whatever happened.

They sat quietly, and she said, 'Oh God, I'm tired.' He hugged her for a long moment, in a close, new, comforting way, and said, 'I'd better set the alarm; I've got an early call tomorrow.'

'Are you going to kick me out?'

'Darling, when have I ever kicked you out?'

Interpretation was misleading, understanding was a trick. Especially tricky for those who are dedicated to superficial contradictions.

'What is the time. . .no, don't tell me. Do you want to sleep? Will we go to bed? Can I use your toothbrush?'

What side of the bed do you sleep on? Do you always sleep on the same side? Do you ever wear anything to bed? What time do you usually get up? Do you wake up before then? Can you do that all night? You smell so good. What did you say?

26

After-glow

Vita put down her drink and powdered her nose, which was practically a political demonstration in these parts. She'd taken a chance, staying on, presuming that a little social mingling might offer a glimpse of something vivid or bizarre. She should have left with Catherine, who'd shot out of the theatre before the applause ended. Never stick around when it's all after-taste and no after-glow.

You'd think she'd have known that by now. The crowd was dense between her and the door. Greetings; introductions; conversations blended, an abstract sonority. The women in this group wore several earrings and matching looks of earnest concern. Serious. These were serious times. The relationship between theatre and politics, the politics of the relationship. The male myths, the phallocratic manipulations, the politics of women and theatre. The women nodded grimly and sipped.

Life was probably more vivid elsewhere. There was, for instance, that rather seedy nightclub in her own neighbourhood. She was feeling homesick.

She looked around. She saw Brian Castle. He saw her, too. She moved towards him and he met her halfway.

'Hello,' she said. 'How nice. You do being a successful young actor very well. It suits you.'

'I think it does. Did you like the show?'

'This is my favourite part. Did you like the show?'

That smile; their conspiracy; the memory.

'It's lovely to see you,' he said. 'How long has it been?'

'Ages, but I've thought of you, which even an actor's ego must adore.'

' "Ages" sounds a bit excessive, darling.'

'Well it has been. We are practically old friends, or something.'

97

'It's nice to have a bit of permanence in a temporary world.'

(Those eyes; they were definitely his best feature. We had a good time, didn't we? The look held longer. Maybe it could still be good.)

'But only a bit,' she said. Her long-ago fascination with him was casually laid between them. It seemed to bear no relation to anything. 'Now tell me, how are you getting ahead without any scandal? Where are the hot items, your private life, linked names?'

'I keep my scandals very private. What are you doing these days?'

'Am I still meeting strange men in hotel rooms? Or is my life once more an open book?'

'That's not what I meant. Whatever, you're looking wonderful,' he said, not at all put out by her reply. That self-possession again, that puzzling charm. The charm defied reason and defied overlooking.

'You always did say the right kind of thing.'

'I wouldn't want to stop now.'

'Don't. Shower me with compliments. Over a drink.'

'I catch your drift,' he said. 'Let me get you a drink.'

The intention might have been a private talk over a drink. The result was instead a diversion. Getting drinks created diversions. Other people entered the exchange. There wasn't another moment for secret smiles, secret contradictions; it only mattered for a moment.

There is time for everything, a new conviction she cherished. Vita soon left and swung onto the street, with the unreasonable certainty of one who knows there's always a taxi about to cruise by.

What I love about everything, she thought, not forgetting Brian, is that sooner or later it seems to be just what you need. The thought took her all the way home.

She'd left the light on, it looked as if everything were aglow and waiting. Those cushions look exactly right just there, she thought; the perfect size.

The flat was just as she'd left it, and it was welcoming. She could simply step back into the mood she'd been in when she left, a nice mood to come home to.

Might as well get changed, stay up a while. Maybe listen to some music, or perhaps wait till later—it's nice when all is quiet, too.

She poured some cognac, a present to herself. It must be addictive, this feeling of being essentially rather faithless. Without creed, allegiance, attachment. Such a beautiful colour, the voluptuous gold, mellow and sensational even before you drink it. Well, without the obvious attachments—religious, political, romantic. But what she'd just called faithlessness required the most binding commitment. Which was a kind of attachment.

Held up to the light, the drink revealed rich depths to the gold; and she saw lines and patterns in the glass that changed with the angle. Glass could be so beautiful. Sometimes you see something really special and you just have to have it. What she'd just called faithlessness was the choice she felt chosen by. It was a choice of an extended world of possibilities. It included opposites and contradictions and outlandish conjunctions. It meant that even the most witless and tedious moments in another breath could turn everything hopeful and enthralling. And not stop there.

The taste was also golden. The frosted stem had its own pattern of tiny lines hidden inside. She was glad she hadn't bought the first glasses she'd seen. You should always wait for exactly the kind you want because then you *get* the kind you want.

Was that true? She would have to find out. Time would tell. Time tells everything, time changes everything.

Was that true? Of course, time changes everything, relentlessly. 'And still,' she said aloud, 'moments in time can continue to be always mine.'

That time she had first met Brian; the way she lived then. It was weird to think of rushing out at any hour of the night in response to a phone call. It had been interesting, no doubt about that. It had challenged and tested her point of view on everything. And taught her so much.

Endings and beginnings never announce themselves. You look back and realise you can pick any number of points as a beginning.

And sometimes you think of something that you've paid no attention to for a while, and you realise with a shock, it's over! And you could call that the ending.

It was definitely getting late, or why would she be thinking this way? These 3 a.m. questions, the ones you keep making up new answers for.

Well, it had been interesting seeing Brian again tonight. She had wondered how and when she would, and now it had happened. Time passes and things change and different things have taken most of your attention. Things that once were important now seem like only a means to the next stage.

Another drink? Maybe a bath. When was she getting up tomorrow? Better find out the time.

And find out again what is ending and what is beginning; if time does change everything; if irony always has the last word; if love really is the answer; if her story has a happy ending.

CODA

'Tomorrow sex will be good again.'
Michel Foucault

I

'Been kissing any frogs lately?' Lindie asks me today.

It's an old story but it's true, you've got to kiss a lot of frogs to find a prince.

'No frogs,' I say. 'No kissing.'

We are sitting on Catherine's terrace, eating lobster and salad. Lindie drove me here with my bags and we stopped at the fish shop, the fruit shop, the bottle shop, the newsagency, and the bottle shop again. Today is bright and clear, and from Catherine's house you can see the whole length of the beach; you can hear the waves and the crowds. It's all mine for a month.

'Well, Vita,' Lindie says, 'this'll be a good month. Nice work, mate.'

What work? We're just lucky. We live in a golden age. We have friends who travel with their good jobs with the ABC and lend us houses by the sea and we can buy lobster and wine and we even have the kinds of jobs we want sometimes. We feel so good, living in a time that myths will be made up about and people will wish they'd been there.

We finish our wine and lay towels on the cool tiles of the balcony and slide to the floor and take off our clothes. Our skin is warmed and stroked all over by the sun. We drift into our dreams, the soundtrack is a hedonistic roar.

These are *our* beaches and *our* beaches are free and safe. Everyone gets brown and hot, then they go in the water, then they eat ice cream, fish and chips, Lebanese rolls. The heat burns away their troubles and the water washes away their cares and the ice cream fills them with the simple, selfish content that is their right in this country. Even people who don't speak English are part of the crowd at the beach, and there is pleasure enough for everybody.

Later, we shake ourselves alert and wrap ourselves in sarongs and I make some coffee.

Today we have a luxurious mood of satisfaction and we say we're doing all right. 'We've got jobs!' Lindie sings, to a popular tune. Usually we complain about our struggles.

There are now shadows on the beach; people are leaving, others are arriving. Everyone in this city comes to the beach on a day like this, and if you're not at the beach on a day like this your life's fucked.

Tomorrow I'll get to work. I'll work well here and maybe I'll also write a play, or at least start one. I tell Lindie my plans: to swim and write and eat health food. Being madly in lust with this actor, she doesn't think my agenda is complete, so we have one of those conversations...

'How about a surfer,' she suggests, 'a beautiful, blond, young spunk.'

'No,' I say, 'none of that for a while. No spunks.'

'What then, sublimation?'

'Seriously, sublimation.'

'Is that a good idea?'

'Maybe there *is* this amount of personal energy that you can turn into surfing or writing or sex.'

'But sex can be an inspiration.'

'It can be a dissipation.'

'I've been told I should use it as a form of meditation,' Lindie says. I remember; this was one of those Orange-people group things she went to for a while.

'Is the other person meant to be meditating, too?' I'm not really asking.

'Oh, all creative people have a struggle with their sexuality.' She seems to be thinking of someone else.

'Unlike other people?'

'Some people,' she says, 'put a lot of energy into everything, plus they can be really highly sexed.' I say nothing. 'What about whatsisname?' she asks. My secret lover, ex.

'I'm not seeing him any more. He is like that—what you said. Lots of energy, loves sex, but a bit indiscriminate, I fear. He has huge energy for his work, too.'

Lindie likes the idea that sex releases the flow of energy. 'When I'm *up* and working well and relating well and feeling good about myself, I'm most sexual.'

'But, you see, you call that *sexual*. Why? It's just energy. I don't think they would always have called that sexual.'

'They never used to be open and honest about sex.'

'No, maybe it's just this modern thing that everything is sexual.'

'Everything is, isn't it? I'm a Scorpio.'

'Like whatsisname,' I say. 'I think sex to him is his only form of relaxation, his only form of intimacy. The rest of the time he's on the phone/catching planes/taking meetings. So it's nothing to do with love or personal relationships. It's a substitute. He was great in bed, but.'

'Can you have sex without love?'

'He loves fucking.'

'I'm just not into those men,' Lindie says. 'I need real contact, sharing, communication. We've got to be friends.'

'What I'm thinking about, you've got this idea circulating because of Freud. Freud is good for pointing out the unconscious motivation of everything, but otherwise he's bad. He said everything was supposed to be sexual sublimation and now everyone believes it. But what if sex is the sublimation for other forms of energy?'

'Why not? Better than eating too much.'

After Lindie goes, I unpack and move the table away from the wall. I clear it and get my typewriter out, all ready. The table was covered with art books and old magazines so I look at them all night. There is Third World music on the radio as I doze off.

2

TEN TIPS FOR BEAUTIFUL HEALTHY SKIN

Cleansing	Protection
Diet	Skin-test
Exercise	Sleep
Water	Facial
Relaxation	Sex

'Everyone's favourite method of relieving stress and reviving energy, sex at its best combines the benefits of aerobic exercise with the ultimate mental/emotional high. Another bonus—sex revs up your circulation and increases breathing capacity, both of which are great for the complexion.'

3

'I had to do this test script and I passed so now I'm writing an episode and then, who knows, I might write for television for the rest of my life. The series goes to air soon. Okay, so it's set in the future and this future is all robots, computers, machines and warring galaxies. Yeah, I know, but I thought it was great at first: fantasy! imagination! adventure! I had to think it was great to get the job. Then I get my scene breakdowns and I start writing and I think: this is the future? These obsolescent adolescent futuristic fantasies? This might be dangerous, because what if through this kind of fantasy we are actually creating this mechanical future where the goodies still win through superiority in physical combat. It's like, that's what the vision is, and if you accept this vision then you support the belief in developing that way. Muscly white men rescuing pretty girls in long dresses.'

'As long as it's entertainment.'

'I mean, what if you didn't have fancier telephones but you had better telepathy? What if besides space travel there was time travel, astral travel? What if the other galaxies had angels and gods, like the ones that came and showed us how to build the pyramids? I tried to say something like this at the last meeting. But I wasn't the one writing the storylines so would I please stick to them and if I wanted to get philosophical I should not be writing for television. Drama, they want, not angels.'

'I thought slaves built the pyramids.'

'And I don't own TV stations or ad agencies; this is my first job here; did I want to go and be an artist instead which does not pay $1500 plus a script, so stick to what we're talking about; we're talking storyline here: do the kidnappers come from the same planet as Fagadi the Terrible? Are they a front for his wicked imperialist plans, or are they freelance intergalactic terrorists? No, honestly. You wouldn't watch it, so I'm not spoiling it for you.'

'Tell me when yours is on, though.'

'Be an artist, they said, just like that, it's true; artists are seen as wankers in a country where they aren't censored or jailed. But that's another story. Well, maybe all this is just an excuse to put off working. So I thought I'd just go and have a swim and a cappuccino and I ran into you.'

'I might have another one, then I've got to work, too.'

'My last job was to write a story on midnight-to-dawn jobs and I stayed up for ten nights and it took another ten days to write and the magazine folded and I never got paid.'

4

Joe came over today. When I first met him in Melbourne he used to be called John but he came to live in Sydney and changed to Joe. 'The streets smell of sex in Sydney,' he explained when he moved up, in the 'seventies. I ran into him in the health food bar, where I would have a carrot juice and get some salad to take home.

He's minding someone's flat, just up the road—Judith's flat; she's away for a bit. I saw her last week, walking along the beach at dusk in one of those priestessy, flower-childy, Arabic things she wears. She was drifting along the water's edge as if she were being carried by the breeze, her silky drapes flapping around her like sails.

'So 'fifties,' Joe said, admiringly, when we got here. He'd just been shopping and had a bottle of wine in his bag, but mine was cold as it had been in the fridge. It was exactly the same wine. I love Frascati, it reminds me of last summer and the summer before. We opened my bottle first and talked about summer, sweet, sensual summer. I told him about my job and he told me about going to all the casting agencies. That's how he'd met Judith. We sat outside and admired the beach. The surfers were down our end, there must have been raving ecstasy in their wordless heads.

'You could do yourself some good here...' Joe began.

'Don't you start,' I said. 'Today a dream surfer, tomorrow waiting for phone calls.'

We watched some guys park their vans in the street below us and peel their wet-suits off. Those bodies. We stared at them on the waves and listened to the screaming from the beach. You always hear that yelling: kids running, being dumped by the waves, and burying their fathers in the sand. Don't mothers get buried? I must investigate. It's nice to have a neighbour in my temporary new neighbourhood but I told him not to interrupt when I was working.

5

Joe knows he's good looking. He looks for a winner, his attention is the prize. He gets ready for a night out and he takes care; he puts on the shirt he always gets lucky in and takes a firm hold of his intention. 'Psyching up.'

Casting spells. An invocation: I'm irresistible, come and get me, I dare you. Check the reflection. Great. You're gorgeous.

He pays for the taxi and wonders if he knows the driver's face. When he stops to get cigarettes a man in the shop watches him. Anywhere he goes in this city, any shop or street or audience, there's someone he's made it with; those whose faces he's seen and might not have seen. That's how I planned it, he thinks. In the city and the bars and the beaches I brush past men I never really see, I don't know who they are, and we have sex together—in the backrooms of bars, in bushes and lavatories, and at parties; in my own bed, in posh big apartments and poky little rooms. I have conquered a long-ago fearful self, and reduced to welcome banality the danger and wickedness of my new knowledge. It started rare and shadowed and clumsy and now I'm the same, but another, person: so cool, so hot, head high, come on over, I dare you. When the signs are right, it's tonight, drinking gin, toking and snorting and sniffing between stations. Want lots, fast and exciting, finishing at the peak. Leave each other at the best moment, leave the car, the backroom, the upstairs, leave his place if he lives close by, and we're back so soon, walk in together and we won't look at each other; we'll go to other ends of the bar and will have picked the next one before the barman has given each of us our separate change.

6

'I've been to a one-day session on meditation,' Joe told me when he came round.

They had different sessions and speakers and they practised meditation and ate delicious vegetarian food.

'This amazing man,' Joe said. 'I don't know if I'll be able to tell you what he said.'

Joe tried to explain and I tried to grasp it. It was about chakra, these flows of energy in your body, and each has a different sort of energy and is linked to a stage of physical growth. 'Some of these chakra are there when you're born,' Joe explained, 'and some open up at a given stage of your life. Like, to a lot of people, seven is an important age and one of these chakra opens then. It's not a physical thing.

'I don't know how they know this,' Joe confessed. 'I don't even know if it's true. The way the guy explained it made it seem true. Anyway, it's an interesting idea. I went to the session quite sceptically, feeling quite depressed and wishing I hadn't promised to go. Halfway through I went to the toilet and there's a mirror and I see my face and it's relaxed and smiling. You just believe in it all for the day; it seems wonderful and important. You don't even notice you're not smoking.'

We exchanged some thoughts on smoking and moved out to the balcony. It was one of the humid, cloudy days, the water murky, fewer people, more seagulls. Charmless birds, seagulls. Why can't there be flamingoes?

'Then he told us about the chakra that opens at about puberty. Each chakra has a biological or physical aspect and then another one. Or, I think, there's a stage of physical development and there's a stage of chakra development. At puberty, biologically it's sex, and the chakra that's ready to open is the kundalini. This is the energy that rises in meditation or when you're very, you know, "spiritual". You know, when you're fifteen and you're full of all this intensity and feeling, all this expectation and longing? God, I'm still going through puberty, are you? I shouldn't smoke so much, I suppose. Okay, I'll finish this: this might not be quite what he was saying, it doesn't sound like it, but anyway. . .you're told it's sex, just sex. When you're that age you're offended to be told these feelings are "just sex". You know you're expecting *something*. Even if it's all expressed romantically, and by being in love you know it isn't just sex. Later you think it probably was. Though if you're fifteen these days you've probably believed for years it is just sex. He said, it's the awakening of kundalini energy and you're ready for your spiritual development to begin. I hate saying spiritual. But now no-one has any models, there's no-one to guide that. He was getting onto needing a guru, but I could never have a guru, could you? Anyway, I hear the age of gurus is over. I don't know what age it is now. That group thing is very Seventies, isn't it? What? Oh yes, models—he said there are all these models around for sexuality but no models for the other thing. Except the gurus or something. So the ego attaches to sexuality; you identify with your sexuality. Remember we talked about this? You know, you think "you" are your sexuality. No, I don't any more

110

either. But these kinds of parallel energies, sex and kundalini, both need models. So kundalini gets dissipated by sex and becomes dormant again.'

Joe said this was not depressing, however, because you can meditate and kind of restructure your brain and catch up on the developing you missed out on by thinking everything was only sex. You have to do a lot of it, though. 'I loved doing the meditation there,' he said. 'It is easier in a group. It's probably mass hypnosis. I have to say I felt something really amazing but I'm not sure what it was. It's supposed to get easier if you do it every day. I wish I'd started the very next day, but I didn't. I think I'll try it, though. But when I sit down I think it's going to be boring or I need a cigarette. The man said when he began meditating he had these most erotic visions. Apparently that happens, I've heard that. Even the gurus go through this stage. You just sit through it and eventually it goes away. It's because of the non-physical chakra you're developing being linked to sex as its physical side. Maybe it's just because meditation is boring and human beings are like apes: they get hornier the more bored they are. Have you got any dope? I'd love a smoke. I should go then. Or I might go to the Gelato Bar, do you want to?'

I really did need some coffee.

'I don't know,' he said, 'maybe it really was the kundalini.'

7

I tap away at the scripts, filling in the story lines, like children's colouring in. Maybe I will write a play—a real play. It could be set in the future. It's my play so I can make up the future. If it's not this TV future, then what? I think about that, and find myself pacing around. Fancy saying, 'This is the future'. If a parable is taken literally, 'warnings' (evil futures) are seen as prophecies that fulfil themselves. You usually find golden ages in a mythical past and dark ages in a mythical future. I find myself now less interested in a futuristic utopia. I would not want my future created by devotees of the 'new age', you'd spend all your time at weekend workshops, comparing past lives. If I went to a past-lives therapist in a future life I'd find out about this life where I was an Australian woman called Vita who went to the beach, drank coffee and made phone calls. Would it be worth fifty dollars to find that out?

I'd prefer the past-lives therapist to tell me I'd been a black-haired, insomnious, chain-smoking, whisky addict; unresting, unstoppable, highly-strung and dangerous. That I'd been treated with fear and diffident admiration; I'd been hard; I'd worn mannish suits and pounded my typewriter all night as an ashtray overflowed and an emptied bottle would join the rest; my plays had been chilling and harrowing and made you blush and cringe and wonder; I'd woken myself with thick, bitter coffee and unfiltered cigarettes; I'd made grown men weep; I'd been frantic and relentless and packed tight every minute because I was rotting inside from disgusting secrets: ulcers, cancers, fear; I'd been ruthless and manipulative and no-one ever saw any tender moments. There was no secret soft spot, no cat no potplant no cherished past love; if anyone stood near they would smell tobacco desperation danger; when I died I'd left nothing behind.

She would actually be thinking of Lillian Hellman.

This is me here. When I wake I wander to the window and gaze at the water. I do salute-to-the-sun and mix lemon and honey in hot water. When I'm sleepy I sit in a hot oil-scented bath and put on fresh white silk. I don't want to write a play today, I feel a bit too healthy. It would taste of muesli. Somehow I finish an episode today. It has no taste.

8

Judith works for Lesley Morrison, a consequential casting agent. It's a good job and one day she could have her own agency. Lesley and some of the actors, producers and directors who come in, say to Judith: 'Stand up! Turn around! Where did you get it? If you made me one, I'd pay you. Call me if you change your mind.

I'd want it shorter, with a belt. Maybe only you can wear those things.'

Judith found out something a few years ago. When she put on her robes people treated her differently. She began to spend more time sketching and sewing. She learnt to make silkscreens and to paint on fabrics. She made her gowns but only for herself, and kept on working for a secretarial employment agency.

She'd been taught at business college to look feminine but not frilly, tailored but not masculine, competent but not threatening. She was still wearing her neat pleated skirts and blazers to work. One day she wore one of her gowns to a new job, wondering if they'd complain about her. It was a week's work at LTD Casting, sorting out files, and they called her back to ask if she'd like a permanent job. Judith was so calm and neat and pleasant. She got things done; without being boring.

Instead of those artistic moods and tears or that constant wide smile that creative people have, Judith expressed her personality through her gowns, her privacy and her dignity.

Actors started to take her aside at the theatre—by now she was getting tickets to everything—and say, 'Love what you're wearing. Doesn't Lesley like me?' Actors who were your friends thought you didn't like them if they didn't get every part.

Lesley and Judith became close friends. Lesley would sit with Judith every day to gossip and complain.

Judith is working the video camera the day Joe comes in. It has run out of tape but Lesley says not to let him know.

She's seen so many actors that day. She has to go through the pretence of giving Joe a test because otherwise his agent complains. Lots of things aren't fair, and Judith's used to hearing that. She includes Joe on the short list to see the director.

Judith and Joe run into each other at the markets; they're both sitting in the sun. Judith's resting her feet and Joe's waiting for a date. He gets her a drink. Some actors are nice to her in case it helps their career. But she takes an interest in him. She likes actors because they're entertaining and selfish and don't make her

113

feel she has to impress or confess. Judith invites Joe to a first night; her usual date has started asking too many questions and hinting he's really bisexual.

At the theatre Judith and Joe meet mutual friends and drink together. Joe leaves with another man, as the men she goes out with usually do. He asks her to dinner soon after, but she knows there'll be too many other people and does not go. She asks him to another first night soon after, so he knows he has no obligations. Soon it is arranged that he can stay in her flat while she has her first holiday in years.

9

I spent the morning cleaning up and getting ready and after lunch I was just going to do some work when Joe came over with a bottle of Frascati.

'I know you work in the mornings. Are you going to have a break?'

It would loosen up my brain for later and I'd have all this uninhibited flow.

He had been cleaning up, too. He wanted to impress Judith in case he could go on staying there when she came back.

'You know what,' he said, 'I probably shouldn't tell you this; I look after her mail and these little booklets in plain envelopes started arriving. I open the magazines she gets so I opened these, too. I think it's probably all right to open just the printed stuff, don't you? Anyway, these were catalogues of sex aids stuff and x-rated videos! Then, another time, I was going through a cupboard, looking for spare lightbulbs, and there were all these videos!'

He watched them, of course he did; he said, wouldn't I? They were just the usual x-rated videos—silly excuses for plots, a bunch of people fucking each other, and 'the standard come shot'.

'Yukko.'

'Did you actually say "Yukko"?'

'Well, did you like them?'

'You don't "like" them but you're not unmoved by them, are you?'

'I wouldn't know,' I confessed. 'I'm scared to look at that stuff.'

I couldn't say what I was scared of: arousal or repulsion. You could turn into a sex maniac or you could get turned right off. I was interested to think of Judith sending away for that stuff. She seems so kind of unsexy—good looking, but unsexy—in those robes and drapes.

Joe enjoys the confessional mode so I hear about his experiences with pornography once we agree there is no such thing: one man's erotica, etc. He said this guy he used to sleep with had a porno-tape of just men and there were tender moments he'd never seen in a 'straight' show. Like, after they'd done all these feats you'd see them give each other a gentle stroke and it was sweet.

What about that stuff he was telling me before? About how sex energy is linked to spiritual energy, so if you don't develop one, you over-attach to the other; if that's how it is. So all this porn everywhere, it really is because of godlessness. Like, people want to behold adore pray worship, but *what*? God is a mild swear word and love is a brandname or a word for sex. So there's sex and it's an appetite that grows by what it feeds on and if it's got no connection with anything it cannot ever be satisfied and so people look for more and kinkier expressions of their exacerbated longing and if that still doesn't satisfy they look for more positions, gadgets and gimmicks and then violence, mutilation and death, because what they really long for is the only thing that cannot be spoken of.

'It doesn't get you anywhere, though,' said Joe. This way of thinking, he meant.

'You know how good it is,' I said, 'to be kind of celibate for a while.'

'No.'

'Not good exactly. But goodish. Don't tell anyone.'

'It's a fad for people to say they're celibate. It usually means they're avoiding something or scared of catching something.'

115

'Aren't you scared of catching something?' I asked. Men have more to fear.

'I think about it,' he said, 'but I don't care. I *do* worry about how my mother would take it if I did. But it doesn't stop me. In fact,' he confessed, 'when the big scare started I was going to saunas even more, obsessively.'

Joe said he would give it all up, the saunas and the bars, if there was one last time that was perfect, couldn't be topped. I asked him his perfect scenario; it included several people and several drugs, videos and opulence.

He asked me mine. I told him I wanted just one person, but everything. True love and anonymity, security and adventure, stability and variety, vigorous youth and wise age, respect and...

'Oh enough,' he said. 'What do you want most?'

'Love and romance.'

'You'll never get it.'

I stopped that right there and went back to the saunas. Was he the only one there?

'No! Sometimes it's even more crowded than before. I don't want to think about why. It's not a death wish. I don't want to die.'

Isn't it thrilling to think that sex is once more linked with death? The man pays. Life, Sex and Death: once more the eternal triangle. The incurable virus is what we have instead of werewolves, vampires and other worlds, connecting sex, mystery and horror. It's our horror movie. The cases we hear of, cures through psychic healing, meditation, visualisation, do we believe them? Is it the evil energy around sex? On the one hand you have 'festival of light' and its fear and loathing; then, on the other, you have leather bars, fist-fucking, mass S and M, that's not puritanism's opposite, it's another expression of fear and cursing, so you create all this hate energy around sex and you end up with a killer disease. But then, not everyone who gets it is like that: puritanical or obsessive. Well, no, but, they connect with this hate energy...no-one knows.

We had drunk the bottle he brought and the rest of the vodka. We went out to eat some spaghetti and talk about food, movies and actors. I'll get up early tomorrow and work then.

10

Ginny rang me. 'Are you working?' she said. 'I hate people ringing me when I'm working so tell me if you are.'

'I was just going to have a cup of tea,' I said. 'Tell me everything.'

'How's the beach?'

'Heaven. I swim every day. I wasn't going to give anyone this number but I gave it to everyone. I'm always swimming or on the phone.'

'Are you getting any work done?'

'Oh yes.'

'I saw that first episode. I was at Maree's and we watched it.' The bitch waited till I said, 'Well?'

'I hated it.'

'Go on.'

'I thought it was dangerous.'

'The mechanical, robotic future ruled by muscly men and that?'

Yes, that was what she meant. She told me more about what she thought and I told her about working in television and the next episodes.

'That's why I don't own a television,' she said.

'Everyone else does, what're you going to do? What else is new? Have you gone out yet?'

Ginny told me she was going to start going out. After years. She rang up her most sociable clients (the horoscopes she cast told her who'd be best to ring) and asked them to invite her to parties. She had lived for ages largely in isolation and only took female clients. Mostly separatists. For a long time she had had little contact with men and none of them heterosexual. She told me she'd been to a party and had had a conversation with a man.

'Hang on while I have a piss and get my tea.' I rushed back to the phone.

'I couldn't believe it,' she said. 'It's as if he had done a course on how to be the old stereotypical man. He kept interrupting me;

117

he would state his credentials if he was losing an argument; he would listen to what I said only to pass judgement on it. How come men like that have survived? He was only the first. I kept finding men like that. I thought they'd be extinct by now.'

'My dear, they are like cockroaches,' I replied. 'You know how only cockroaches will survive after nuclear war. All the poisons and deterrents in the world only cause cockroaches to mutate and become more indestructible. I'm sorry to tell you this.'

'It was as if it was his right to correct me and I should be grateful,' she said.

'Many women,' I instructed her, 'would hardly dare realise if they were less than grateful because of the deeply imbedded knowledge that the male ego is as fragile as it is enormous and if the male ego were shattered it might be the end of the world as we know it.'

'The women at the party were feminists!'

'Don't make me laugh she said mirthlessly,' I said.

'I don't know whether to laugh or cry.'

'Don't laugh,' I said. Then, as a warning, 'If you are going to go to parties and talk to men you need to know that a man doesn't care who he interrupts to get the attention he needs. Don't you read magazines? This childishness men project onto women promoting a myth that it is the female of the species who is childlike. Only man could believe that. This should not be news to you.'

'I'm thoroughly depressed, thanks. I'm going now.'

'I feel great now. I needed this little talk.'

'Good luck in television.'

11

It wasn't the smell of an airless room. It wasn't the smell of a sweaty body. It wasn't the smell of blue cheese or of fish or of rotting fruit. It wasn't the smell of a smoker's morning breath.

Nor of the Vegemite Judith carefully smeared on one slice of toast. It was that other smell.

Her mother would gaily sweep into the kitchen with only her unfastened dressing gown on. Judith would not look at her.

Once she had said, do that up, and reached out to fasten the gown and her mother had moved away and laughed at her. Judith wouldn't say it again but no-one could make her look at those breasts hanging wrinkled and heavy. Judith would be dressed, shoes cleaned, badges polished, belt straight, blazer brushed clear of dust and hair. She would make toast, spread the butter evenly, cut the pieces into neat thirds. She wouldn't look at her mother when her mother hugged her.

The smell. The man had stayed. She didn't know when she had made the connection, didn't need any other sign he was there. Whichever one he was. He changed a few times and twice changed back to a former one.

Sometimes she would have to meet him and shake hands, and he did not smell. The smell was on her mother and in the bedroom when he stayed.

Judith's mother smiled a lot when the man was there and smiled as she tried on clothes to wear when he came, or when they were going out.

One time, when all the ladies came in the afternoon, and there were cakes and coffee and liqueurs, they had to say what they loved most.

'The very most? Just one thing? A thing or a person or...?'

'What you love most,' said Aunt Eva, who wrote for a magazine and practised interview questions at the ladies' afternoon teas or at bridge.

They shrieked and protested and said they couldn't answer: there wasn't any one thing they loved most, or it was a different thing every day, or it couldn't be said in front of the child.

Judith's mother knew what she loved most: men. Men loved her, too, because she knew how to please them. Ask intelligent questions, her mother advised, and he will think you are intelligent. Make him feel important. Don't tell him your troubles. Uncle

119

Jerome now had a separate bedroom from Aunt Eva because when he came home from the office, he works hard, poor man, she wanted to talk about her own troubles first. Your husband won't sleep with you if you do so. Never say no in bed. Don't be as silent, as secretive as you are, my dear girl. It is more attractive to laugh at jokes even if you can't make jokes. Wear the colours that really suit you. Do not talk of your troubles or about the things that don't interest a man, but do talk.

Judith's mother would chatter gaily in company, and she would chatter gaily with Judith, out of habit or for the practice, as she followed her to her room.

'Eat,' Aunt Magda would say. 'Eat, eat; this one is good; this one you haven't tried; this one from the real baker; it is the real cake.'

'She'd better not eat so much,' Judith's mother would say, 'or she will get fat, but whatever she eats she stays the same; I was always the same, but not now, unfortunately.'

'You haven't changed at all,' Uncle Stephen would tell her, and Judith's mother would glow and Aunt Magda would shake her head and Judith would stare and stare into the intricate designs on the embroidered cushions, the painted plates, the reptile skins that covered the ladies' feet, the bright enamel on their toenails.

12

'There was a madam of a famous French brothel. All the generals and philosophers went there; it was the best of its kind and this madam was very famous. In her old age she was interviewed and asked: "Madame, do you have a philosophy of life?" "Why, yes I do," she replied. "It is this: gangsters for sex, queens for company." '

'So?'

'Speaks for itself, really.'

13

Judith knows what Joe would assume; it's what anyone would assume. She goes out with gay men for all the same reasons other women do: because they're there. And the obvious advantages. Look at the alternative.

And they'd assume she has a past of love affairs and that these days she has sex, occasionally, with sailors and musicians and travelling salesmen; with someone she might agree to see late at night when she's back from the theatre and he's back from working late at the office; with married men, schoolboys or taxi-drivers; or whoever else women are supposed to jump on these feminist fag-hag days.

Judith, in fact, is a virgin.

Is there a reason? The connection of personal history to the facts of one's present life is another assumption. It is true that Judith was shy and did not encourage boys' advances. Her first boyfriend lasted for years and, for reasons of his own, did not ever ask her to sleep with him. She was twenty-two when they parted. No-one knows they never slept together; no-one knows a twenty-two-year-old virgin these days.

But now, to tell anyone, that would take on the proportions of a major confession. Men try her but what would they say if they knew? And who should be first? If it were just another one, she too could say: yes, maybe, not yet, on condition. But to him it would be just another one; to her the first. How do you know when to say yes, how do you know when you want to? This is how she'd like it to be: like a dream; unasked and already created. It would unfold itself and fade into mists that are blown away in the light.

She sends off for the x-rated tapes and watches herself watching them, alert for her own reactions. What is this remote, unreal feeling? Is this what people feel? She gets up once, walks uncertainly round the room and sits again. When it is over she puts both cassettes back in their cases and puts them in the cupboard, where her sewing things are, where no-one would go.

She goes from room to room. In the kitchen she opens the fridge door and in the cold light stares at the frosty, gleaming shelves, heavy with bottles, jars and containers.

Back in the sewing room, fabric is stretched out on the trestle; there are pots of paint in one corner of the room. Judith starts mixing some colours. She has already dreamt this one: there will be various greens lit with pale gold and shadowed in purple— these are the curtains for that window in that room and they will take your eye to the leafy trees and there'll be dappled leaves inside and outside.

The colours are right but she is not ready. She takes a shawl and her keys and though it is dark leaves her flat to walk along the beach.

14

I wake from an afternoon sleep of strong, secret dreams that emphasise connections that don't stand to reason.

I start cleaning the house and turn on the radio. There are some kinds of songs that, although you would never buy the record, when they come on and you're alone you stop what you're doing and turn the volume right up. Then you dance, maybe slowly taking off your clothes.

How potent cheap music is. Moonlight on dark waves, breezes on a hot night, and the longing from which it is all born.

The phone. 'Dearest,' I say. 'Nostalgia and now you. How was the tour?'

'I just got back from Brisbane and we went for drives up the Sunshine coast,' M says. 'This country! I mean, this country!'

'I know, I know.'

'The beaches, the rainforests...'

'I know... Even here. Where else do you get a city flat overlooking the beach? Today we were lying on the balcony in the sun and it's a normal working day.'

(Earlier, Joe and I had watched some workmen doing repairs

to the road. It was hot and we were drinking chilled apple cider. 'It's like a French movie,' Joe had said. 'The bourgeoisie discussing art while the workers toil.')

M says, 'In Queensland they lie on the beaches and discuss Princess Di's wedding ring.' He sounds disgusted.

'I know. Same thing. It's so good here.'

'But where is the angst? I kept worrying about this. Don't we need some angst? Because everyone has angst and no-one has this. . .this opulence?'

Lindie rings. 'It's perfect. The sex is great, the relationship is great, everything is great, and I'm not even thinking "What's wrong? There's got to be something wrong." I love my job. I love the pay. I'm so happy. I just need to finish painting the house. I'm having coloured walls. Blue in the kitchen. What do you think?'

Catherine rings. 'Oh good, I'm glad you're enjoying it. I'll be back on time. I have this rather dismal story to tell you. I had an affair with one of the crew. I must have been mad. Things are going to have to change. How's the work?'

Work is the answer to some fundamental question. We most often talk about work, sex and money. Work and sex and money are an eternal triangle and energy is their substance and love is the area they define, but right now I need to think hard about how I'm going to get some money because I don't really like television. First, there were those scripts, and then this stupid, ugly producer thought I'd sleep with him. Like any woman, I think of the obvious way to combine work, sex and money—after all, we all sell ourselves, as they say in television, but that's no longer an option.

Pamela told me that 'in your day there was lots of champagne and hundred-dollar tips but nowadays call-girls are getting straight day jobs to make ends meet.'

In this grim decade there's Fringe Benefits Tax, AIDS, condoms, devalued sex, economic disaster and an oversupply of hookers who haven't been able to raise their fees in years. That's not the usual whoring fantasy is it. More like Parisian courtesans in jewel-encrusted gowns at the Opera.

Anyway, I wasn't serious. Anyway, I've been told I was a temple dancer in a past life. Past lives sound so romantic and I've been told why. This present life will, in the future, sound utterly romantic, too: that's the kind of life people like us choose.

Pamela's since made a lot of money in real estate, but now it's too late for that as well.

Catherine says, 'Weren't you going to write a play?'

Ginny rings. 'Are you enjoying your Venus transit? For most people it would mean a relationship.' We laugh. For me Venus brings only a heightened sense of beauty.

'But I did go on an old-fashioned date,' I tell her.

This man asked me out to dinner. I thought, I'll never sleep with him but at least we can have dinner, why not? I thought, if he chooses a more expensive place than I would, maybe I won't insist on paying my half. When we ordered, he said, 'I'll only have the garlic bread if you do, too,' so I knew I'd better pay.

Soon I'll have a Pluto to Moon transit. When she had one, Ginny says, 'It was like, I looked into the void and found nothing there.'

'I know how that feels!' I say. 'It rained yesterday, and it was so cold. I didn't have anything to wear. I only brought beach clothes, things to wear in hot weather. I didn't bring anything for the rain.'

She is laughing at me again. 'That's how you live your whole life!'

It is true that I have never been one to save for a rainy day. And soon I won't have a job any more.

The phone stops ringing. I've slept in the afternoon so I'll be up all night. I'll write about another life that could have been mine, about the memories by which we know ourselves, about the sequins I'll sew on my swimsuit, about the longing from which we ourselves are born.

15

Joe stands on the corner. He has recognised the chemist and the laundromat and he knows this is the street. He stood on this corner the other morning, looking for a taxi, watching the rosy mists of the faint, first light, and marvelling at the beauty of a pink stucco building.

He walks down the leafy side-street again. It is about two blocks long—a cul-de-sac. He recognises the grey stone building with the flame tree in front. The block he's looking for (an elegant old building, white, bay windows, four flats maybe) should come after it, but there is only that red-brick development of townhouses with the auction sign on the billboard outside.

He's certain this is the street. Okay, so the first time he came here he had a head full of drugs—perhaps that had sharpened his senses. That and everything else. . . those luscious bodies, those men over him and into him, taking him and themselves to the limits of ecstasy, fucking him through the most intense arousal to the most exquisite salvation, fucking him to eternity's boundaries.

He remembers what happened. . .

He had been picked up in a bar. There was only a look, the man had said only 'my place'.

He was taken to an apartment and shown a marble bathroom. Then to a room lined with splendid silk carpets and pillows; each object there beautiful: white lines laid out on glass trays like mandalas, everything to smoke, sniff or swallow. This man must be a millionaire, he thought; he's amazing; this city's amazing. Who *is* he?

When it was over, he found himself on the street, and the fact of early morning occurred to him slowly. It could have been noon or next week.

He went home to sleep and woke immobilised with sadness and remained silent and alone for another day.

But in that dawn he had felt exultation and it was this street;

it had to be. He had reached the corner, just like this, and here seen the main road and known where he was.

Eventually he asks. One woman looks at him, affronted, and hurries away. Joe walks back to the corner one more time and returns, and an elderly man is clipping a hedge near the flame tree. He has lived in this street thirty-five years. Joe asks. The building he describes was there, the man tells him, maybe twenty years ago. They pulled it down to build those rotten townhouses. Sure he's sure. They sold all the townhouses before they were completed and they're crook. Joe listens as long as he's able to a rundown of the changing real-estate values of the street in the time the old man's been there.

16

Judith holds her sick and bloated centre and realises it has been a long time. She is premenstrual and would have her usual sleepless night. She waits for the headache. There is no headache. Her calendar says seven weeks. Maybe she forgot to make a note, not like her; clockwork. But the calendar reminds her of a full and trying week, three weeks ago. Judith would remember if on top of it all she had her period then. Fancy missing one. Maybe she had stress. You take Vitamin B: pills, wheatgerm, beer. Or iron: spinach, fish, eggs.

There's a tampon in her purse and it'll come and she'll feel better.

Then it's ten days later. You don't have menopause before you're twenty-nine, surely. Is she having a worse diet or more emotion than usual? Maybe she's got blockages or deficiencies or cancer.

She has to go back to the doctor's and what he tells her is impossible. There is some failure rate with most methods, he says. What was she using?

This doctor does not know why she says such things. He knows a counsellor. They can talk about termination, she must realise these days such things are easily arranged, there is help.

She goes to another doctor and gets wise. If she tells the truth they'll send her to a shrink, maybe lock her up.

She gets her sleepless night and figures it out. She'll borrow someone else's story. She'll say she is another one who thought it was over and threw away her method and then he came back for just one last night then went to South America.

She won't show forever with what she wears.

Then it's a few months later and she's telling Lesley she's leaving. Lesley rages and lectures and tries to talk sense.

Some girls would kill for a job like this. What it can lead to. Judith needs a longer holiday, though in this business everyone works hard; you've got to be tough; let's face it, no-one appreciates that without casting there isn't a show. Does Judith want to work part time for a while? Think about it a bit longer? Have a week in Bali? They could plan a future for her. To leave, just leave, what's *with* Judith? Is it some crazy idea to do her own thing, make those djellabas and nuns' habits for a living? NO? Lesley gives up then. Oh well, if Judith's made up her mind... We'll miss her and where will we get anyone else for fuck's sake.

Judith locks up her flat and takes her grandmother's wedding ring and another borrowed story.

In a country town she can be another deserted wife and supplement her pension with alterations and mending. A woman from pre-natal asks her to make a frock, but Judith says only if there's a dress to copy from.

One night, though it is not yet time, an ambulance comes. They put something over her face and she breathes in and goes far away.

Her hands are pressing on her flattened stomach as she wakes. She wakes and does not know what day it is, if it *is* day. Women come to her in stiff white dresses, their hair covered.

Judith struggles to see. 'Where,' she tries to say, 'where is...' There is nothing in her room but her own high, narrow bed. There is silence. There is no sign of new life. The white women say, 'Hush, take these.'

They move silently in and out and beg her not to talk.

They give her things to swallow with water and she floats and dreams and watches them come and go.

Another woman in a stiff white coat comes; she takes Judith's hand and gently asks her questions she does not understand. She recognises the words but they do not make sense so Judith tells the doctor what she knows: how to pour paint onto fabric so it looks like the rain falling on the sea, how to see that each colour contains all colours, how you can tie one piece of cloth into a turban or a veil or a sling to hold a baby.